Praise for *The Courtesan's Keeper*

'Sanskrit literature is today associated only with philosophical writings ... so it comes as a refreshing insight that a thousand years ago, a poet in Kashmir wrote a treatise on the life of a courtesan' —*Asian Age*

'Brutal in execution and frank in uncovering the underbelly of social life, it contains ... wisdom that can stand contemporary scrutiny' —*Tribune*

'*Wife of Bath* and *Kama Sutra* meet eleventh century witticism in this translation'—*First City*

'The book has been translated superbly, to the audience of this time' —*Brain Drain* blog

PENGUIN (●) CLASSICS

THE COURTESAN'S KEEPER

KSHEMENDRA lived in Kashmir circa 990–1070 CE. His literary output over at least three decades includes still-studied works on poetics and prosody, apart from devotional and didactic verse, mordant social satire and a lost history of the kings of Kashmir. Eighteen of these works were recovered in the past century, and sixteen are known through citations. They have established Kshemendra as a prolific and multifaceted writer on a wide variety of subjects and an important name in classical Sanskrit literature.

ADITYA NARAYAN DHAIRYASHEEL HAKSAR is a well-known translator of Sanskrit classics. Educated at the universities of Allahabad and Oxford, he was for many years a career diplomat, serving as the Indian high commissioner in Kenya and the Seychelles, minister in the United States and ambassador in Portugal and Yugoslavia. His translations from the Sanskrit include *The Shattered Thigh and Other Plays*, *Tales of the Ten Princes*, *Hitopadeśa*, *Siṃhāsana Dvātriṃśikā*, *Subhāshitāvali*, *Kama Sutra* and *Three Satires from Ancient Kashmir*, all published as Penguin Classics. He has also compiled *A Treasury of Sanskrit Poetry* which was recently translated into Arabic and published in the United Arab Emirates as *Khazana al-Shair al-Sanskriti*.

The Courtesan's Keeper
Samaya Mātrikā

Kshemendra

Translated from the Sanskrit by
A.N.D. Haksar

PENGUIN BOOKS

An imprint of Penguin Random House

PENGUIN BOOKS

USA | Canada | UK | Ireland | Australia
New Zealand | India | South Africa | China | Singapore

Penguin Books is part of the Penguin Random House group of companies
whose addresses can be found at global.penguinrandomhouse.com

Published by Penguin Random House India Pvt. Ltd
4th Floor, Capital Tower 1, MG Road,
Gurugram 122 002, Haryana, India

First published in English by Rupa & Co., New Delhi 2008
This edition published by Penguin Books India 2014

10 9 8 7 6 5 4 3 2

ISBN 9780143421474

Typeset in Adobe Caslon Pro by R. Ajith Kumar, New Delhi

Printed at Manipal Technologies Limited, India

www.penguin.co.in

This is a legitimate digitally printed version of the book and therefore might not
have certain extra finishing on the cover.

P.M.S.

For my brother
Sushil
with love

Contents

Contents

A Note on the New Edition

Kshemendra's *Three Satires from Ancient Kashmir* was well received when published in the Penguin Classics series in 2011. *The Courtesan's Keeper* has now followed suit. Titled *Samaya Mātrikā* in the original, it is perhaps the finest of the satirical works by this brilliant, once-celebrated but now little-known writer. Written with candour and compassion, it spotlights both a face of Sanskrit literature and of life in Kashmir, almost totally unfamiliar to readers today. Though virtually a thousand years old, it can still ring bells for present-day enjoyment. The publishers are to be congratulated for bringing it out for public view once again. My thanks in particular to

R. Sivapriya of Penguin India for this new edition and its elegant presentation and to Richa Burman for its editing. I have also taken the opportunity to make some corrections in the texts of my introduction and translation.

New Delhi,
Republic Day, 2014   A.N.D.H.

Introduction

The present is the approximate millenary of Kshemendra, the celebrated writer in classical Sanskrit from eleventh-century Kashmir. Little translated, he is practically unknown to readers in other languages. An important part of his work is satire. This is a genre comparatively rare in Sanskrit literature and seldom associated with it in the current common perception of the ancient language as one mainly of religion and philosophy. A droll, observant account in it of Kashmir a thousand years ago would be rarer still.

The foregoing seemed sufficient reason to bring *Samaya Mātrikā*, one of the finest of Kshemendra's satires, before today's readers in the present translation, the first into English as far as known. Other reasons were: the sheer readability of this novella about a courtesan's life; the light it sheds on human propensities and on the social and other conditions of the time; the snapshots it offers of Kashmir; and a perspective of Sanskrit writing provided in the simplicity and the irony, the humour and the innate compassion of its vivid descriptions of people and places.

*

Before elaborating on the book, it would be fitting to introduce the author. Unlike many writers from ancient India, Kshemendra has left some personal details in his various works. Collated by modern scholars, and cross-checked with other sources such as Kalhana's history of Kashmir, the *Rājataranginī*, they provide an outline, however minimal, of the man's life and work.

Much of Kshemendra's productive life corresponds with the reign of King Ananta (1028–1063 CE) in Kashmir. This king is named as the ruler of the time in five of his works,[1] including *Samaya Mātrikā*. A sixth[2] names the king's son and successor Kalasha (1063–1087 CE). Scholars surmise that the writer was perhaps born before, then educated during, the time of Ananta's grandfather, King Sangramaraja (1003–1028 CE). Though his own dates cannot be pinpointed, they are estimated as roughly between 990 and 1070 CE.

Kshemendra came from a cultured and affluent family. His grandfather Sindhu, perhaps the same as a high treasury official of this name mentioned by Kalhana, may have founded the family fortune. His father, Prakashendra, was a wealthy and pious man who devoted himself to religious rites and philanthropy. While describing these, Kshemendra refers to him with warm respect and gives a tender account of his death in ecstasy while at prayer.[3] His own son Somendra continued the family's scholarly tradition, making an addition to one of his father's later works and also providing further details about him.

Given this background, the kind of education Kshemendra received is not surprising. He mentions studying literature with the foremost teacher of the time, the famous Shaiva philosopher and literary exponent Abhinavagupta,[4] who was active in Kashmir till about 1015 CE. Two other teachers he names are the poet Gangaka and the preceptor Soma. The second appears to have initiated him into Vaishnava studies.[5] A third was Manjubhadra or Viryabhadra,[6] a distinguished scholar from Nepal, with whom he studied Buddhism. His erudition was thus both vast and varied. The two ancient poets he has eulogized are the sages Valmiki and Vyasa, traditional composers of the *Rāmāyaṇa* and the *Mahābhārata*. His early work includes verse abstracts of both the epics. Devoted in particular to the author of the second, he frequently uses the epithet Vyasadasa, the servant of Vyasa, for himself.

Apart from his forebears and teachers, Kshemendra has also named others who occasioned his writings. The two abridgements of the epics were prepared at the instance of his friend, the brahmin Ramayasha, and a third at that of Devadhara. The Buddhist monk Nakka encouraged his later compilation of the *Jātaka* stories. A well-known work on poetics[7] was composed for Udayasimha, the son of his friend Ratnasimha, the ruler of Vijayapura. This prince, himself a poet, is also mentioned by Kshemendra as his student and quoted by him in a separate work on poetry.[8] Another student he quotes there is the prince Lakshmanaditya.

Though he had princely friends and students, Kshemendra does not seem to have sought or received royal patronage, as was the case with many men of letters in that age. Perhaps his own resources precluded any such need. While he refers with due courtesies to the king of the time in some of his works, in others there are no such references at all. Eulogies indicative of patronage are also totally absent. The overall impression is that of a scholarly and meticulous man of independent means, who engaged himself in literary and intellectual pursuits for their own sake.

*

A century and a quarter ago, Kshemendra's work was known only through references in Kalhana's *Rājataraṅgiṇi* and in some anthologies. Its first manuscript discovered in modern times, by A.C. Burnell in 1871 at Tanjore, was that of his third abridgement, of Gunadhya's lost *Brihatkathā*. In the succeeding half-century, Indologists G. Bühler, A. Stein, P. Peterson, S.C. Das and M.S. Kaul, at different times, located manuscripts of his other works, mainly in Kashmir. So far, eighteen of these have been located and their texts printed.

Another sixteen are known, at least by title, from references and quotations in these texts, but still remain to be found. A list of these is appended with the endnotes.[9]

Of the now available works, three are the already mentioned abridgements, respectively of the *Rāmāyaṇa*, the *Mahābhārata* and the *Brihatkathā*. Academic opinion considers them the fruit of the early years of Kshemendra's literary career. The last mentioned bears a date corresponding to 1037 CE. Three other works deal with poetics and literary criticism. They are still regarded as important contributions in these fields, apart from providing valuable information about other Sanskrit writers. Four are satires on contemporary life, among them *Samaya Mātrikā*, which also contains a date corresponding to 1050 CE. Of the remaining eight, five are didactic works on conduct and policy, and one a compendium on daily rites.[10] Finally, there are two devotional works: Kshemendra's long poetic account of the Buddha's good deeds and former lives, dated to a year corresponding to 1052 CE, and his shorter verse narration of the ten incarnations of the god Vishnu, dated to 1066 CE and regarded as the last of his known compositions.[11]

The sixteen works known only through reference or quotation include some plays and long poems, a satirical novel, a possible retelling in verse of Bana's *Kādambari*, and what appears from the title as a commentary on Vatsyayana's *Kāma Sūtra*. There is also Kshemendra's history of Kashmir, the *Nṛpāvali*, which is described by Kalhana[12] as 'the composition of a poet', but decried as full of errors.

A contemporary scholar[13] has attempted a description of a number of these so far unlocated works with some interesting details culled from available quotations and references. It is to be hoped that a search for them will be pursued, so that at least some can be brought to light in coming years.

The existing Kshemendra corpus reflects a prolific and multifaceted writer. In the tradition of earlier Kashmiri savants, like Anandavardhana and Abhinavagupta, he was both a notable poet and a seminal theorist of poetry. While modern scholarship has generally lauded his contribution as manifold and important, it has tended to emphasize the historical and literary significance of his work on poetics. But a wider view has also been expressed. For K.M. Panikkar,[14] 'Kshemendra was perhaps the most comprehensive mind of his time, who wandered in every field, including satire, with distinction.' For A.K. Warder, he 'stands in the front rank of satirists' and 'invites us to enjoy the multiple contrasts between the idealised or rather morally balanced world of legends and the bitter reality of contemporary society ... for these we must recognise him amongst the greatest *kavis*'.[15]

*

The title *Samaya Mātrikā* can be translated literally as 'Little Mother by Compact'. She was an older woman, usually a retired practitioner, often a relative, who stayed with a courtesan to act as her chaperone, guardian and manager. Another word which Kshemendra uses for such a person is *kuttani*, indicating a madam, bawd or procuress. She is the principal character in this tale, recounted in 639 verses grouped in eight chapters of varying length.

The narrative begins in Pravarapura, the principal city of Kashmir at that time. It has been identified by modern scholars with the site of Srinagar, the present-day capital. Kalavati, a young and beautiful courtesan there, is in distress as her guardian, who was also her grandmother, is dead and her business is suffering as a result. She confides her worries to her friend Kanka, a local barber, who advises her to get a replacement. He also recommends one whose life story, he says, will be highly educational for her.

This story is narrated in the second chapter of this work. The present name of its protagonist is Kankali, but it was different at her birth and changed many times in the course of a colourful career and many travels. During these, she moved from place to place within Kashmir, eventually going out through a mountain pass in Pir Panjal to the plains below. Many of the places where she lived have been identified through academic research and provide a fascinating glimpse of the continuity in the historical geography of Kashmir. Their details are also appended with the endnotes.[16]

Kankali was born in Parihasapura, a former capital city, and was the daughter of a woman who minded the grindstones at a local inn. A pretty, precocious girl, also given to stealing, she was put into the flesh trade by her greedy mother when she was only seven. As a young woman she shifted to a nearby town where there was no dearth of customers, but eventually robbed a temple after a tryst in its sanctum with a palace guard. Fleeing to another town, she became the concubine of a wealthy country squire and the mistress of his property. After engineering his death, she took up with his son, resorting to witchcraft in the process. But she soon moved to a mountain shrine, posing as a widow engaged in performing religious rites for ancestors.

She then lived with a rich, old knight and so conducted herself at his death as to be treated as his wife and officially given possession of his assets. This was followed by an affair with an official, whose house she sold with a manipulated court order despite resistance from his sons. However, alarmed by their attitude, she moved to a convent where she resumed her former trade. Jailed for dealing in stolen goods, she escaped after sleeping with the jailer and fled once more to another town, this time living as a Buddhist nun. Here, she became pregnant and then returned to the capital as a wet nurse for a minister's child. Quitting the job when the child fell sick, she lived thereafter as a cattle herder, a cake seller, a naked holy woman and a porter, among other occupations. Eventually she left Kashmir to wander in the plains, passing herself as a person of great age and esoteric wisdom.

The third chapter describes, with colourful pen pictures, the quickening of life in the city's bordello quarter as dusk falls. In the next, Kankali appears in person, brought by the barber Kanka, to meet the troubled courtesan. A skeleton of a woman with conspicuous teeth, she accepts Kalavati as a daughter and proceeds to give detailed advice illustrated with stories from her own experience. This continues in the fifth chapter which lists eighty types of passions that need consideration while dealing with men.

The sixth chapter is a counterpoint to the third. It is morning time and Kalavati is escorted by her new 'mother' and the barber to the top of her house to survey the day's market. Various possibilities are pointed out, including an officer on horseback and an envoy from a southern kingdom. Finally they settle on Panka, the young, inexperienced son of a rich local merchant.

After an agreement is negotiated through the barber, Panka comes to Kalavati's house in the next chapter. The bejewelled youth is accompanied by seven voluble parasites, looking for some benefit at his expense. Kankali first has to deal with these characters, who include an official, a drama teacher and a doctor's son, among others. There is a party before Panka is taken to Kalavati's bed.

In the final chapter, Kankali arranges to get the parasites out of the house with a hue and cry about a theft, and threatens to call the police. She then visits Panka's father in the morning and inveigles a large sum from this moneyed and miserly trader. Finally, she persuades Panka to sign legal documents to provide for her ward's future. Kalavati's interests assured, it only remains to drive this young lover out with insults and threats of his getting involved in a murder charge.

*

The story depicts a vibrant and diverse society. Chiefly urban, it is also relatively stable and harmonious. Its mix is liberal, ranging from the busy courtesans and their adjuncts in the foreground to the affluent and the indigent people, and from intellectuals and workers to the upper crust and the humbler classes. There is, for example, a minister seeking religious ordination, a rich moneylender trying to ward off supplicants, and a porter who carries loads along the trade route to the plains. There are priests who resell temple offerings, monks who fornicate on the quiet and doctors who may be quacks. There is an elaborate functioning administration, though some officials make fortunes during the time of the autumn harvest, when tax is collected, and others are susceptible to bribery in the court. On one hand, there are country magnates of substance and retired knights, cavalry officers and poets, accountants and shopkeepers; and, on the other, there are modest flower sellers on the streets, liquor vendors, beggars and bandits.

Women move about freely in this society. They inherit property and litigate in courts. The heroine is a rich cattle owner at one time and the respectable widow of a gentleman at another. She is also, by turns, a roadside mendicant's companion, a living goddess and a soothsayer. Her career displays an awareness of the world outside Kashmir. The story refers to Turkish and Chinese people, apart from those of Gauda and Vanga in the east Indian plains. There is mention of the great cities of Varanasi and Pataliputra and of the west Indian kingdom of Malava, whose ruler is represented as maintaining an envoy in the valley.

Kshemendra also describes the habits of the people. Both women and men are depicted as wearing jewellery and dyeing their hair. They drink wine, eat fish and mutton, and chew betel leaf, a luxury imported from the plains. Cloth from China is held in value. Parties and festivals are popular and frequent. People visit temples and shrines, convents and monasteries, though also for purposes other than prayerful. Many believe in charms and amulets, spells and witchcraft, and many are attracted to holy personages, or those pretending to be so. Religion sits lightly on others, who do not hesitate to joke about gods and goddesses to make a point.

It is in this lively setting that *Samaya Mātrikā*'s story unfolds. The principal characters are an attractive courtesan, her shrewd old keeper and their customer, a naive youth. Each is drawn in vivid detail, as are the lesser figures: the experienced barber, the avaricious merchant, the loquacious parasites and the pert servant women. The events mainly take place in the courtesan quarter of the capital city and are described in picturesque detail.

*

The Kashmir of *Samaya Mātrikā* is also known from other works. Kalhana's *Rājataraṅgiṇi* was written just a hundred years later, and it is supplemented by other literary and archaeological evidence. By 1050 CE, the turbulence of the early years of Ananta's reign seems to have given way gradually to peace and prosperity. The valley bustled with old and new towns. Trade and agriculture flourished. Travel to and from other regions may not have been as frequent as in earlier times but was still considerable, specially on the southern salt route,[17] so called as there was no local production of salt and it had to be regularly imported.

The presence of many temples and Buddhist monasteries indicated the active religious life of the people. Ananta and his consort Queen Suryamati were both devotees of Shiva and built temples and endowed foundations in honour of the great god. A temple to his son Ganesha is mentioned in *Samaya Mātrikā*. The work begins with invocations to the goddess Kali and the god of love, Kama. Kshemendra himself appears to have been a devotee of both Vishnu and Buddha, as we have already seen.

It was also a time of substantial literary activity in Kashmir. Somadeva, a younger contemporary, followed Kshemendra's abridgement of the *Brihatkathā* with his own retelling some thirty years later for his patron, Queen Suryamati. This work, the famous *Kathā Sarit Sāgara*, is generally considered much better reading than its predecessor, though it may be less faithful to the lost original.

Among Kshemendra's other junior contemporaries were the writers Bilhana, author of the biography *Vikramānkadevacharita* about a king in south India, and Mammata, the rhetorician who wrote the celebrated and still-used work on poetics, *Kāvyaprakāsha*. Two others were Kshemaraja and Bhaskara, both students of Kshemendra's old teacher Abhinavagupta and well-known commentators on Shaiva philosophy in separate works. From these and other details, it would appear that Kashmir was then far from being a cultural backwater as in later times, but was rather 'in the vanguard of Indian culture with notable contributions to every aspect of its life'.[18] *Samaya Mātrikā*, a product of that period, reflects the ebullient age in which it was written.

*

A comparison of Kshemendra's numerous writings with the criteria of literary excellence and propriety spelt out in his own dissertations on poetics would be a fruitful field for academic research. Another would be the analysis of any evolution in the language and presentation of his works which span a period of three decades. *Samaya Mātrikā* belongs to the middle of this period and may thus represent a talent already matured.

23

A reader of this work cannot but be struck by the directness and economy of its style. Though it contains some scenic and allegoric descriptions in the conventional manner, the elaborate ornamentation of the *kāvya* genre of this period is largely absent. The narrative is terse and the pen pictures, brief and sharp, sometimes brutally so. The action is generally fast-paced, except in one chapter where it gives way to didactic classification.

A notable feature of the work is Kshemendra's frequent usage of unusual words and compounds, some unavailable in the standard Sanskrit dictionaries and others whose meaning occasionally needs to be inferred. This affects the easy comprehensibility of his language which nevertheless provides a contrast to the general writing of the period and its conventional idiom.

*

The present translation is based on the texts of *Samaya Mātrikā* brought out by Osmania University, Hyderabad, in 1961 and by Chowkhamba Vidyabhawan, Varanasi, in 1967.[19] The former contains an explanatory appendix, invaluable for any student or translator, of difficult words used by Kshemendra; and the latter a Hindi commentary and notes, also helpful, though it is difficult to agree with some of the conclusions. I have also profited from the account of *Samaya Mātrikā* given in Dr A.K. Warder's monumental *Indian Kāvya Literature*, and the monograph on Kshemendra by Dr Braj Mohan Chaturvedi. For a background of the period I have relied mainly on Dr S.C. Ray's *Early History and Culture of Kashmir* and Kalhana's *Rājataranginī*, translated with notes by the late R.S. Pandit. Other useful works are the pioneering *Kṣemendra Studies* of Dr Surya

Kanta, and a more recent study of Kshemendra by Dr Uma Chakraborty.[20]

My translation endeavours to combine fidelity to the original with the requirements of modern English usage. Most of it has been done in prose to maintain narrative continuity. The stanzas in the prologue and the epilogue, and a few others which contain descriptions in the *kāvya* style, have been rendered in verse. Some of Kshemendra's chapter headings have been rephrased for better understanding, and one devised for chapter six, which did not have any in the Sanskrit text. Mythological and similar references in the text are explained mainly in the endnotes; but some phrases have been added in the translation in a few cases where it seemed necessary. A few verses have one or more lines missing in the text, and these I have left out.

To translate Kshemendra has been a

challenging and fascinating experience. Apart from its reflection of the human condition, his satire also conveys some colour of his homeland as it was then, and a tinge of his own personality. This brilliant and versatile writer deserves to be better known and I hope more of his work can come before today's readers through other translations.

*

I would like to thank Sanjana Roy Choudhury for her ready response which encouraged me to complete this translation which I had begun several years ago. Thanks are also due to Sushma Zutshi of the India International Centre Library, who enabled my access to the original work and a variety of reference material, and to Sunil Kumar Sharma of the same library, who photocopied the Osmania

University text for me. I acknowledge also the work of Pushpanjali Borooah in copy-editing the typescript. For my wife, Priti, who patiently read and helped improve the drafts, and supported me in so many other ways, no words of gratitude can ever be adequate.

Noida,
Independence Day, 2007   A.N.D.H.

Prologue

Homage to Kama,
whose power is wondrous:
with a bow wrought of flowers
and a breeze as the arrow
he conquers the world.

Reverence to Kali,
awesome, majestic,
enchantress of all.
Her age is unknown,

at the end of time
the world will be seen
swirling around
in her fearsome mouth
like a little fish
in an angry sea.

This work, *Samaya Mātrikā,*
giving the secret stratagems
and all the tricks of courtesans,
is written by Kshemendra.

A Worrying Question

In Kashmir, there is a famous town called
Pravarapura.[1] Its name is a byword for worldly
pleasures. A jewel upon this earth and the
abode of all delights, it is a place for every
kind of enjoyment for gentlemen. It is well
known as the playground of that amorous god
who is the personal guru of its young women.
For Kama, having abandoned the rest of the
world for fear of Shiva's fiery eyes,[2] lives in
the delicate loins of these ladies about town.

In this town lived a beautiful courtesan
named Kalavati. A true source of Kama's pride,
she surpassed even the moon in radiance. One
mascaraed glance from her was enough to
entrance any man. The dark glint of her eyes,
the arch of her brows and the thrust of her
bosom were ample evidence of her vocation.
One day, as she stood on the roof of her house,
she saw a certain barber on the street below.

This barber was a mentor to all the
courtesans and a cheerful companion for their
customers. He had bright beady eyes and was
as plump as a cat which feeds on lakeshore
frogs in autumn. His face was covered with
whiskers, but his big bald head was like a
burnished copper pot: with just a ring of hair
along the sides, it was a butt of jokes for all
the men about town.

Afraid that someone might spit on his
head, the barber looked up and caught the

eye of Kalavati, who signalled to him with a
glance to come up. Going up to her, he was
surprised to see that her gaze was dull with
worry. 'What has happened?' he asked, putting
aside his usual flirtatious banter. 'Your hair
hang undone, your eyes without collyrium,
your lips aquiver with sighs, your face sunk
in thought! The lively bird inside you is silent
and still, as if asleep. Why are you looking like
a wife whose husband has gone away to some
foreign land?'

'The girdle around your lovely hips always
sang the praise of Kama,' the barber continued.
'Why doesn't it tinkle a welcome? Why aren't
your limbs made up as usual with extracts of
sandal and camphor, bright as Kama's glow?
Did you spurn some great profit in the hope
of getting one even greater? Or are you feeling
cheated by some long-enjoyed blandishments
which turned out to be false?

'Is it that a thief gave you some matchless jewellery fit for a king, and you were greedy enough to take it without any thought? And then were so careless as to flaunt it before your colleagues who have chattered about it to the city's Chief of Police?

'Or is it that there was a wealthy man always ready to give you money, so that it was generally believed that he was especially attached to you? But his friends and relatives were opposed to this, and they found an opportunity when you humiliated him, which so put him off that he went and got himself married?

'Has some fellow, who once gave you a bit of jewellery or a dress but then distanced himself, now got you in his power like a fierce evil spirit which takes possession of some popular watering place?

'Or did some rogue, who could not gain his ends by gifts of money, bewitch you by secretly sprinkling magic powder on your hair, even as you fled from him, changing course like a fish in water?

'Have you willy-nilly got into trouble on account of money? You were promised some, but were greedy to get more, and now have only a deep grievance within your heart? Perhaps you ignored a merchant with long-term prospects and exulted instead in a liaison which was no more than a flame on a twig. And then, when the fine new dress is in tatters, and the old one no longer there, you lose the benefit of both?

'Is it that a very rich patron, whom you had pleased and persuaded to give you an endowment, has been enticed away by some envious woman? Or have you been dropped by some hugely wealthy person whom you had taken the utmost trouble to cultivate?

35

'Or have you become faint and indifferent? Turned off pleasure? Gone deaf and blind because of some distraction? Is all well, my dear, with your infallible art and skill in handling lovers, even on the difficult path which knows no rules? And, my sweet, are your charming airs and coquetry, which can stoke passion to a peak as they prepare the ground for amorous sport, as good as ever?'

The barber was a well-wisher and a friend in joy as well as in sorrow. The courtesan was distraught with worry and fearful of the loss of her livelihood. On his inquiry, she heaved many a sigh and said: 'I'll tell you all, Kanka, about the never-ending anxiety which is consuming me. Because of it, I am wilting like a flower in the heat of summer.

'Friend, my mother's mother has been murdered by a wretched doctor. She was as stiff-necked as an elephant and couldn't move about much, but she guarded this house and its treasures like a she-serpent.

'This doctor Rogadhara knows the secret sciences, but he is arrogant and always bent on instant termination of cases. He is also mad for money, which keeps him young though he is an old man. He gave me some savoury medicine, two-thirds of which was finished off by my grandmother in a fit of gluttony. Then she fell sick and began to see the whole world as made of gold. It was a conspiracy by our enemies, this obsession with gold, and it killed her. Even in her final moments she saw the earth as golden and kept saying, "Take it, child, take it."

'Her passing has devastated my house. Prospective clients treat it with contempt and trespass at will. I am being overrun by them just as a deserted inn is by travellers on the road. Those who are broke, but strong, will not leave. Those with some money get no opportunity to come in. I do not like this free-for-all situation. How can I bear the same treatment from those who care for me and those who don't? So, I want to go away to some other place.'

After listening to her tearful account, the old barber tried to console the courtesan. 'My lady,' he said with a sigh, 'for the sake of money you let in this wicked libertine of a doctor so very thoughtlessly. He has killed the mothers of many courtesans with his medications. Didn't you know that he is notorious, and known as the death of all madams? When he sets out, hunting for the sick who are his prey, the dandies and their servants greet him with the prayer addressed to Yama, the god of death.

'Now stop grieving and calm your mind. You need to arrange for a professional mother. If there is no madam, looking like a tigress for flesh and blood, customers become shameless and impudent, like jackals.

'Courtesans are always busy with this or that. There is no respite for them without a mother. Not even for the half hour at daybreak or dusk. Rogues leave their houses no more easily than does a cat asleep under the oven in winter. Rakes enter the house in their finery but begin telling tales when asked to pay. A young courtesan without the mother is like a garden of flowers without a hedge of thorns, or the wealth of a kingdom without guardian ministers: all at the mercy of libertines and their henchmen.

'Lotus-eyes, this is the time for you to earn money commensurate with your good fortune in having such lovely breasts. One should never let a flowering vine wither away. The days of youth are fickle rascals. They embrace you and go away for good, never to come back again.

'Therefore, proud lady, you need to find a mother adept in every stratagem for augmenting your earnings. Such a person is as important for enriching young courtesans as is the autumn harvest season for tax collectors. In the selection of customers, she must be like the many-sided balance of time, on which even a mountain can be sized up and cut down.

'Listen to the account of one such woman, a supreme adviser and dispenser of rules for the unbridled pleasure seeker. Through her hands all courtesans can attain their goals. Just listening to her story can give one a special understanding. To get her advice in person would be akin to having the whole world at one's disposal.'

The Story of a Life

Kalavati was all attention as the barber recounted the madam's story. It was a veritable encyclopaedia of sharp practices. 'I tell you this tale,' he said, 'after homage to that all-consuming goddess in whose womb rests the triple world. In the old days there was a roadside inn for travellers at Parihasapura. A woman named Bhumika minded the grindstones there. She had a daughter named Gharghara Ghatika, which meant a "little gurgling pot".

'This child grew into a pretty girl. But she was a thief. Invited by the townsfolk for religious rites on feast days, she would steal the receptacles used for the puja. She was also precocious and could speak maturely to people by the time she was seven. Then her greedy mother put her up for sale at the market gateway under the name Jalavadha.

'With time, her body filled out. Her bosom swelled within the bodice, her throat acquired the curving lines of a conch shell and her limbs the grace of a tender vine. She began to entertain the men about town with hugs and kisses. Eventually, she enticed a merchant's son who had come to procure saffron. Purnika by name, he was young and handsome, with a rich complexion and plenty of gold on his person.

'Attracted by her flashing eyes and amorous glances at a gathering, Purnika was filled with desire. He came at night for a tryst with this flirt, and when he was drunk and asleep in her arms, she quietly took off and hid his gold ear ornaments. Pulling off the gold rings from his fingers, she then started screaming that she had been assaulted by a robber. The merchant woke up with a start, but it was he who had been robbed. Ashamed at being seen by his friends, he covered his face with his cloak and beat a hasty retreat.

'Thereafter, the young woman began to live in Shankarapura. She had by now acquired fine clothes and jewellery, and assumed the name Malhana. Good luck came her way in abundance. She collected lovers like flowers and found no rest from fornication, day or night. Entering or leaving her house, or just waiting outside, these lovers soon became as numerous as street dogs.

'During the day she would devote herself to reliable customers, equally at a well or a watering place, a garden or an eatery, a flower shop or a friend's house. At night she would begin by putting a drunken client to bed like a baby, then go to another and, when he was fast asleep after lovemaking, to yet another. Giving the excuse of having to go to a sick girlfriend's house, she would proceed to yet another. Such were her constant rounds among the many who purchased her favours. Pursued by others who were annoyed with various pimps, she would flee and hide in the house of some other lover.

'The palace guard Nandisoma was madly in love with her. One night he brought her for lovemaking into the sanctum of the goddess Gauri's temple where, when he slept like a log, she took all the ornaments off the divine idol and quickly slipped away.

'Assuming the name Nagarika, she then became the mistress of one Samarasimha, a country squire who lived in Pratapapura. An excessive diet of meat made her fat, yet he loved her like the hero Bhimasena loved the ogress Hidimba. After gaining control over all his property, she wanted him dead and, with this in mind, incited him into a conflict with his kinsmen. And, when they had all perished and the property was in her possession, she became the concubine of his son Shrisimha.

'By this time her youth had faded. To bring Shrisimha under her influence, and also to undermine his wife, she resorted to witchcraft. She devoted herself to stuffing her young lover with fish broth, ghee, milk, onions, garlic and other aphrodisiac foods every evening. But, fearful of a neighbouring ruler who had begun to threaten the new squire, she took as much of his money as she could and moved on to another town.

'There she changed her name to Mrigavati

and took to wearing the thin, white garments of a widow. Assuming a modest air with eyes downcast, she also began to evince interest in almsgiving. She would go with some sacred *kusha* grass, sesame seeds and camphor to the temple of the goddess Sureshvari on the bank of the Shatadhara spring and spend long hours performing rites for ancestors. At that place of pilgrimage, she hooked an extremely rich knight named Bandurasara, just as a crane snaps up a fish.

'Adept at captivating the minds of men, she soon got a grip on the knight's household and began controlling all his income and expenditure. Within a month, this wealthy man passed away, and she sat clasping his feet as if intent on following him on to the funeral pyre. Prevented by his kinsmen from persisting in this course, of which she had put on a show, she spoke to them with the profound forbearance of a well-born woman.

'"In a noble family," said she, "widowhood can carry the stigma of unchaste conduct, which may be considered as the cause of my losing my husband. All this will be expunged by the fire." And as evidence of her grim resolution, she sat silent and still like a rock, though this impassivity must have been due to the expectation of coming into more money.

'Well, on the orders of the king she was given possession of her husband's wealth. The royal officers begged her to live on, which she agreed to do, pretending it was only at their insistence.

'She took up with the clerk of the equine stables. To make love like a mare was no more than changing the name by which people knew her, from Mrigavati, a doe, to Ashvini, a filly, which also denoted more passion. She would meet the clerk in the bathhouse, and with her ministrations and dissolute conversation, she stole his heart. He rolled about all day amidst his birch-bark dossiers and after eating and drinking to his fill, slept like Kumbhakarna at night. It was only in the mornings, when his drunken fevers had been calmed in the bathwater, that he could do justice to the coital techniques of which he was so proud.

'Mrigavati was growing old. She made it a point to please and humour the clerk and, selling the entire livestock from the stables, took possession of the proceeds. But he also had sons, and when they prevented her from also selling his house, she went to court. There she seduced the magistrate and bribed the court officials who got together to arrange a fraudulent disposal of the property, so that she won the case and obtained possession. She then sold the house and appropriated everything it fetched.

'But she was afraid of the clerk's sons. So, disguising herself in another garb, she took refuge in a convent of the Shaktas—those who worshipped the Great Goddess. There she darkened her grey hair with a dye and became a young, new courtesan once more. The word spread that a merchant's daughter-in-law had taken residence at that place. This improved her vendable aspects, as people love a rumour and rush to it one behind another without considering whether the substance of the story is true or false.

'Soon her hands and fingers, lips and even tongue were worn out with the drunken clamour of suitors. Still she took passion to its limits, again and again. Once, despite her attempts at concealment, she was caught by some villainous servants while receiving stolen money. She was arrested and put in prison in fetters. There she took up with the jailer, who lived up to his name: Bhujanga—secret lover. They enjoyed themselves endlessly, feasting on fish, cakes and wine. One night, in order to extricate herself from the passionate embrace of this man who was drunk and smothering her with kisses, she bit off his tongue. Unable to call for help, he fainted with the pain, whereupon she threw off the fetters and covering her face with her shawl, promptly escaped from the prison.

'She reached Vijayeshvara the same night. There she declared she was Anupama, the daughter of a high royal official. In earlier times, her youth with its varied beauty had helped her in the pursuit of pleasure. What little remained of it, she now decked with jewellery and make-up. Her breasts were thrust up artfully, her hair decorated and her eyes lined with kohl. When she came out thus, with a red sash tied to her wrist and her face covered up to the nose with a veil, many were entranced and wondered who this new nymph could be. But, after that first, eager curiosity, once they saw her naked, they were turned off and did not return. After all, like a cold room in winter or a lamp lit during daytime or a faded flower garland, of what use could an old and worn-out whore be to anyone?

'She began to put up with the lack of customers. In the evenings she would importune passers-by with her cloak spread out and beg for a little donation. Eventually calling herself Shikha, an ascetic woman, she started keeping company with the penitent Bhairavasoma who would give her half the food he received as alms. And when she herself went out to beg, her body daubed prettily with ash, her eyes enlivened with collyrium, a string of varied crystal beads gleaming at her throat, and her arms and bosom bursting out shamelessly from a tight bodice, she could still throw foolish minds into turmoil.

'While she was living thus, there was a famine and it became very difficult to get food by begging. One night she stole the penitent's money and other possessions and moved on. Describing herself as a victim of circumstance, she went to the monastery of Krityashrama and posed as the Buddhist nun Vajraghanta. There she stayed and meditated with a bowl meant for alms in her hand. Her dress was an old worn-out garment dyed ochre, the colour of false love. Her head had been shaved so that it looked like a pumpkin, and for the sake of a morsel of food, she would let it be patted and stroked by lecherous visitors.

'She had always been adept at imparting instruction in occult practices to credulous people and now, she went from house to house offering to teach wicked ways to women of good families, the casting of spells on customers to courtesans, and multiplication of money to merchants. To the foolish she would also give charms and talismans, and thus came to be held in high reverence by all.

'After a while she was confronted by a living obstacle to her pretensions—an unexpected pregnancy which was the result of her liaison with a devotee's servant, Mangala. A swelling belly put an end to her livelihood and after childbirth, she gave up religiosity, put on a wig, and went back to the city.

'She was lucky enough to be engaged as a wet nurse by the wife of the minister Chitrasena who had just had a son. Here she came to be known as Ardhakshira, as half the milk needed for the newborn came from her. With the baby in her arms, she would sit on a cushioned throne-like seat, looking as though she was waiting to devour the whole house, though she received rich and nutritious food to preserve her supply of milk.

'Fate made her the recipient of great comfort in the minister's house. Nourished by a good diet, her aged frame was rejuvenated. Her arms became rounded and thick with flesh. A necklace of corals adorned her throat, and a pair of silver rings her ears. The woollen wrap suspended from her ample hips quivered as it rubbed against her ankles.

'But due to her carelessness, the minister's child caught a fever and she was told by the doctor to give up eating fish broth and to fast instead. "Unwholesome food should be avoided," he said, "not to speak of rice. As a caring wet nurse, drink only *amla* juice for two or three days. You can enjoy good things and all kinds of feasts again once the baby gets well."

'But the doctor's advice fell on deaf ears.

Her feelings for the child were no more than for a twig. Seeing that he was very sick, she pitilessly removed his gold birth amulet and ran away that very night.

'Thereafter, she set up house in a border region with a herd of goats on a pasture. Here she prospered and became well known as Dhanavati, a rich woman. But then there was a cloudburst and heavy rainfall in which the whole herd perished. All that she was left with was herself and some hides. Leaving them with a herder, and taking a heavy blanket of his as security, she proceeded to Avantipura where she assumed the name Tara and became a cake seller.

'She would buy a basket of the small cakes offered at the shrine of Ganesha and then heat and sell them on the street every day. But those who look for large profits eventually lose their original capital, and this happened to her.

Reduced to eating leftover rice thrown out by housewives, she got hold of a street urchin, a girl whom she anointed with ghee and called Kushalika. She started going from house to house with her, begging for money, which she falsely said was needed for the girl's impending marriage.

'Taking on the name Panjika, she began to stand in front of gambling houses and secretly sell loaded dice. As the flower seller Mukulika, she also peddled remnants of floral and other offerings at the temple. One night, however, she decamped with the bounties of the temple guards and went off to a village, where she called herself Hima, a purveyor of water at fairs, and started stealing ornaments off children watching pantomimes.

'Calling herself Varna, she then posed as an astrologer who was able to reverse planetary movements for the arrangement of marriages. Credulous opinion gave her a reputation as an expert in astral science though she knew nothing of it except some names. After some time, she began calling herself Bhavasiddhi—one who could get possessed by a goddess—and would stop speaking except to say "make your offerings". Then she took to acting mad and living naked, caressed by dogs. She became famous as Kumbha Devi—a living goddess—and began to be worshipped regularly by devotees.

'Soon the minister Kuladasa became desirous of getting ordained by her. He made her a votive offering, but she purloined the silver vessels for the ceremony and once again set off.

'Her course, like herself, was serpentine. She spent three days as an itinerant saleswoman, hawking liquor under the name Kala, the distiller. One night, she appropriated seven bells belonging to the ascetic Katighanta who had got drunk and fallen asleep. The next night, she doped some travellers with wine laced heavily with the narcotic thorn-apple and, taking all their goods, got away to Shurapura.

'A porter whom she called her husband was accorded the same treatment on the salt-trade road they were following. When he had passed out at night, she attached herself to some other travellers. And in the morning, taking possession of his load of goods, she moved on. Tightly girding the porter's long rope around her ample middle, she carried the load on her head all day in great spirits.

'Traversing perilous hills through barren, steep and snow-covered paths, she reached a place called Bamba as the day was ending. It was autumn, and though she had a thick and large blanket, she was suffering in the cold. Covering her face with her sash like a respectable woman, she timidly sought refuge in the monastery of the Panchalas there, on the edge of the border.

'Leaving Kashmir, she then travelled all over the world which is girdled by the island-studded sea, declaring she was an old and learned brahmin lady named Satyavati. Everywhere she went, she contrived to become an object of reverence: at one place as an adept in yoga; at another as an ascetic on a month-long fast; and at yet another as one on a holy pilgrimage. Winning the confidence of fools by seeming to reveal what in fact was well known, she gained tremendous acceptance, especially in the homes of the landed gentry. "I will stupefy your enemy's army," she would tell local rulers and, availing of their treasure, would secretly leave at night before any battle could commence. To the affluent, she would speak of sacred places: the waters at Kedara, the funerary rites at Gaya, the holy baths in the river Ganga and suchlike. Giving them relics and amulets allegedly from these places of pilgrimage, she would relieve them of their money.

'Her advice was sought even by highway bandits. They wanted to learn the science of divination of hidden treasures and carried her around in a palanquin during the rains, till she fled from them. She also took to giving, for a price, fennel seeds to her disciples saying that they were sacred *rudraksha* beads whose merits she extolled. Other devotees, who believed in subterranean passages to the netherworld and were eager to consort with the nymphs who dwelt there, were pushed into deep wells after being robbed of their clothes and jewellery.

'Occasionally she claimed to be a snake charmer, tying a string of smooth and slippery toxic pellets around her neck and declaring that her limbs were suffused with venom. At toll barriers, it was her practice to give the tax collectors flowers which caused momentary hallucination, and then pass through them.

"'I am more than a thousand years old," she began to say. "I know the science of alchemy and am adept at all kinds of speeches. The essence of all that is desirable in the three worlds lies in the palm of my hand." Crushing their regard for all other gurus with such arrogant and limitless claims, she brought gentlemen *thakkuras*[1] down to licking her feet like dogs. Such was her trickery that the Kamboja chiefs sang her praises and the Turushkas exhausted themselves in her service. Could the people of China do otherwise? As for the Trigartas, they were beside themselves in eagerness to wait upon her. The people of Gauda took pains to do the same and, with flowers in their hands, so did those of Anga and Vanga.[2]

'Thus did she traverse the land, right up to the sea, going from strength to strength with her deceptions and stratagems. Eventually, when her energy and strength began to flag, she came back home. For who can give up one's own land? It is like one's own body, even though withered by age.

'Now she calls herself the daughter of a king who lost his throne. Her fingers are stubs and her teeth all gone. Her nose tip was bitten off and her forehead is covered with black spots. But she knows the ways and the words of all countries.

'I alone recognized her,' the barber concluded. 'She is like a snake which guards the treasures scattered within a house. If this mother of greed were to become your house-mother, my beauty, then consider all the wealth and riches of suitors to be in your hands already without further effort. This being the case, for your sake I will go myself and request her to become the stepping stone to your success. She is a crooked fraud but she knows everything. What more can I say? She understands how to win the world by wit, and there is no other alternative.'

After narrating all of this to Kalavati, the well-wishing barber quickly took her leave.

Life Begins at Dusk

Dusk was falling as the friendly barber got ready to go and fetch the courtesan matriarch, a woman wicked by nature and the mother of all tricks and expedients. It was the time when pleasure seekers give up all thought of sleep in bravado born out of exertion, shame and the prospective loss of their money.

As daylight faded from the sky, the flaming sun hung suspended for a moment in the evening glow. Forsaken by the fast deepening shadows, it then plunged, fiery but lustreless, into the ocean waters. Darkness arose like black smoke from the incense of aloe sticks which harlots burn. Lamplights came on like champak flowers to adorn the spreading inky tresses of the night maiden. A half-moon appeared, like an ivory comb dropped by heavenly nymphs while quarrelling over lovers.

People are happy when the day ends and the moon rises. It becomes a festive time of love for all. The sky, like a harlot, has no hang-ups: for it, the long-enjoyed wealth of sunshine is now no more than a memory, and it swiftly adorns itself with the glory of the moonlight. Rakes on the lookout for liquor begin wandering casually in front of courtesans' establishments. The madams inside are glued to the doors, all ears for the slightest knock in their keenness to land a catch. As for the girls, they sweep away the garlands and betel leaves left behind by daytime visitors and decorate their beds as they await new arrivals.

Reclining on couches, some of them invoke Kama with a tinkle of their anklet bells, echoing the chirp of his favourite bird, the pigeon. One flirts with a client already enticed. 'Why didn't you come earlier?' she asks. Another quizzes the madam. 'You already took an advance,' she says, 'why are you taking it again?' And when some local toughs, their long hair knotted and with cloaks tied around their bellies, begin an argument, yet another girl, who has taken advance payments from two or even three of them directly and also through her madam, quietly slinks away.

Some women mourn a double loss when a new arrival is turned back in anticipation of a known client who fails to materialize. One placates a customer, who has had his turn but is prepared to pay for another, by blaming her madam. 'What can I do,' she tells him, 'if that good mother of mine does not know a sweet man like you? What is the point of my living now?'

These crafty women are quick to propitiate simple-minded visitors who are generous in every way but angry at always being ignored. But the madams shout at impostors and conmen who try to gain entry under other people's names. When a fresh customer arrives, and the house is already full of lechers intoxicated or exhausted and asleep on the floor, the courtesan will often take the newcomer to the house of a girlfriend. On the way, she will of course ogle another suitor, pretending that she is calling out to a kitten.

'One is already inside,' another courtesan tells her mother madam. 'Another has also arrived. Yet another is insistent on tonight. What shall I do?' The old woman gets ready with some stories to while away the time, knowing that the night is long, the suitor callow, and her girl very young. 'We don't accept payments from unknown persons. There are too many foreigners singing and wandering around.' But others may make such remarks out of embarrassment at having an empty bed in the house.

When an obviously indigent visitor is audacious enough to barge in despite being stopped, some courtesans pretend a headache or a gripe in the stomach and begin to cry. But simple-minded and free-spending so-called friends are praised and lauded by the procuresses as they are a constant source of profit. In the presence of a first-time customer, a paid scoundrel will say to the courtesan, 'My beauty, I am ashamed at the little money I have, for you are worth ten times more,' or, taking a wealthy client aside, the madam will tell him, 'My girl has been reserved for the son of a high official who is on holiday,' and extract from him three times the usual fee.

'I've never seen you before,' another madam tells a visitor, 'besides, this is too little for my daughter and there is no time today.' But all this while, she holds tight to his cloak and will not let him go. 'Please excuse my girl just for this night,' says yet another while fobbing off an infatuated but completely broke suitor, 'for she has been taken away on a date by the minister's son.'

The girls also talk amongst themselves. 'That salesman came today, but would not pay me as he had missed his turn,' says one. 'That terrible general will become my enemy if he does not get time,' adds another. 'What happens to my earnings from the temple if its manager is not provided his special favour?' the third exclaims to a friend as she takes her turn with the garden basket for shopping. 'Other women,' they say, 'can spread webs of trickery to attract the money of simpletons. What can we do? We know nothing of deception and such arts. That man is always suspicious of everything. It is his nature to get turned off when one is nice to him.' Such is their talk while they fleece simple folk.

The lovers talk too. 'That whole delectable night passed in a second. But it was just wretched entertainment!' cries one agitated and exhausted customer when the others teasingly question him. 'And I was in agony all the time,' he adds, cursing the crookedness of the courtesan's cunning and disagreeable keeper. 'That girl never came to bed at all!'

'Such libertines can have no entry to our house on days when men of merit come here to amuse themselves with conversation and suchlike,' says one courtesan in a loud voice to put in their place those who tend to assume airs. 'It is only at night that we must somehow entertain these lechers for our livelihood.' Nevertheless, 'Taralika, put on your necklace!' 'Manohara, your pair of bracelets!' 'Leela, look to your girdle!' 'Chitra, don't forget the sandal paste!' 'The night is reaching a climax!' Thus, like proficient teachers, the friends advise each other.

Kankali

She arrived with the barber as dusk fell, like darkness with night. A clever procuress given to talking with all the town's scoundrels, she looked like a ghost, a skeleton held together with sinew and topped with a skull. The stomach was sunken, down to the gut. The body—a bag of skin with holes—was just a cage for the bird inside, a bird capable of teaching deception to the whole world.

She was like a measuring rod for this age

of Kali, calibrated a thousandfold to take stock of everything and everyone. Even after swallowing up all that there was, her jaws always gaped wide for more. Like a medley of notes in a tune put together, she could be opulent for the wealthy, sinful for the wicked, and vile for the base. Thus, she had been made.

Her appearance was dreadful. The long, pointed teeth were clearly visible, like those of a bitch in painful labour. The face was like an owl's, the neck like a crow's and her eyes like those of a cat. It was as if each limb had been drawn from creatures that are always at each others' throats.

For courtesans a guard unique,
she could make their suitors take
to crutches after rites of love—
like the dark smoke swirling up

from lechery's sacrificial fire
which blinds those men with tears.

Kalavati got up hastily on seeing her. Greeting her with due ceremony, she bowed at her feet and seated her on her own seat. 'For courtesans like us, you personify the three divine qualities of creation, preservation and dissolution,' she said. 'In imparting instruction you are like the four-faced Brahma, in creating cunning illusions like Vishnu and in fighting off penniless suitors like the great Bhairava.[1]

'Doe-eyed girls may offer the freshest delights of Kama with their beauty, brilliance and the enchanting flush of youth. But without your advice, they can never accomplish their purpose.

'Consider me like your own devoted daughter, seeking refuge and having nowhere else to go. The wise are always kind, even at first sight, to those who surrender themselves to their care.'

The visitor called herself Kankali, a name that meant 'a fleshless skeleton'. From Kalavati's entreaty she realized at once that a good opportunity for a comfortable living was at hand. 'My girl,' she replied, 'your affection has won my heart. Even without having carried you in my womb and suffered the pangs of labour in giving birth to you, I consider you my own child. This barber recommended you to me. He is a lifelong friend who has many a time stitched my nose when it was bitten by libertines. You are fit for the gods, and alone worthy of my counsel. It is only on a proper surface that pictures can be painted to attract the eye.'

'With time and constant practice,' Kankali continued, 'you will acquire the entire wealth of artful skills. But first of all listen, child, to what I have to say for your own good.

'Money is dearer than life. It comes from neither lineage nor conduct, neither learning nor beauty. To acquire it you need brains. And they are a rare commodity for most. This world, I know well, is full of mindless sheep. They have no idea of what should be done at a given time, and suffer day and night as if they were sick. Leave aside humans, even the gods and the denizens of the netherworld are wanting in intelligence.

'Look at Brahma, so venerable and yet so thoughtless. What did he gain by making the youthful beauty of a woman's breasts as momentary as a flash of lightning? Where was the wisdom of this foolish god of creation in putting oil in the tiny sesame seed but not in the pumpkin? Or wool on goats and sheep but not on the elephant?[2]

'And look at Vishnu who wanted the precious gems of the ocean. Why did he take the trouble of getting it churned with a mountain peak? He could just as well have conjured up a beauty full of make-believe passion to loot all that treasure in advance. Then his slumber, his dependence on the goddess Shri, his hauling of the earth as a load, his mendicancy, and excessive expansion or absence of all attributes: are these appropriate for a god who is called the best?[3]

'As for Shambhu, with a moon which is always waning, attendants who go naked, and a wife who grabs half his clothes, I do not know what purpose is served by his friendship with the god of wealth. His limbs are smeared with ash like an ascetic, but he flaunts a woman on his lap for all to see. Is this proper? He calls himself detached, but fools about with hordes of ghouls. Is this being true? Is it sensible for the supreme lord to be going about on a bull, and wise to make a show of the subtle skills which should be kept secret?[4]

'Look at Surya, the sun god, so able and always on the move. He loves to dally with women, but why does he dim his light? With his riches, which woman would not be ready? For wealth, she would put up with even the most fiery of suitors.

'Then comes Chandra, the deity of the moon. In crescent form he serves the great god Shiva, but his emaciation is never put right. How can the arrogant fool attain fullness when he is sitting on the Great One's head? If a suppliant wishing to better his prospects does not seek place at the patron's feet but, proud of his merits, acts high and mighty, he only harms himself.

'Spring I salute. With its arrival, lovers get kicked about like the ashoka tree and rogues drink up the nectar like bumblebees.[5] But Mara, the god of love? He went during that season to distract the great god with the other sex. But why do so with a bow and arrow? He should instead have spun out the lovely qualities of women. Hence, the dolt just got himself finished off.[6]

'Look at Indra. He is the lord of the world. Celestial sages are his ministers, heaven and earth his dominion and full of great gems is his treasury. He has an ocean of ambrosia, an army of immortal gods and a castle on the divine Meru's peak. The illustrious Vishnu is his friend. Yet the king of heaven's intelligence was such that his whole body is spotted with marks like the cunt.[7]

'The foolish gods! They churned and tortured the ocean, the home of countless treasures, till its anger burst out as bitter poison. Eventually it was exhausted and ready to yield its all. Yet they were fatuous enough to be satisfied with just one elephant, a horse, a tree and some wine.[8]

'Rama's eagerness to catch the golden stag, Yudhishthira's game with the loaded dice, Janamejaya's jealous gripe with the priests— such instances create bridges of folly on the pathways of mankind.[9]

'I cite another example. The nectar of immortality is difficult to obtain, despite the hardest effort. The Nagas gave it away to Garuda. They did not drink it, keep it or even look at it. They lost it simply because of their witlessness. It just shows that in this whole world, no one has even a single grain of real wisdom. All run after money because of the karmas of their previous lives.[10]

'What can simple women do when people are so stupid? We live only by the grace of these fools. They are prepared to believe things even if they see the contrary being done with their own eyes—so tricks and illusions are what harlots must make their money from.

'In the old days, I once spat some chewed betel leaf on the hand of a brahmin called Matharaka. It was a joke, but that ignoramus was so proud of his caste that he took it as an insult. He flared up in public, enraged and bent on violence. "Good sir," I told him, "you have misperceived because of some irritation of the humours. I didn't spit anything at all. Rub your hand on the wall and see for yourself. How can you trust your eye, which is just skin, and not the words of a girl full of warm feelings for you?" and hugging him with an arm around his neck, I swore such strong oaths that he was convinced and promptly returned to his normal self.

'So, you see, men without intelligence are the main support of courtesans. And also of poets and parasites. When I was young, a brahmin's son once came to my house for a night of pleasure. His name was Shankara Vahana. He was just a lad, stiff and strong, very excited and a virgin. "This is a tough fellow," I said to myself on seeing him. "The night will be long and I am already tired out. So I must try to keep him off intercourse." With this in mind, I spent the first watch of the night talking to him and telling him long stories while we were in bed. Eventually, he started saying, "Is there anything else? I've heard this already. Now I am feeling sleepy." To avoid having sex with him since the storytelling was over, I then began moaning as though in pain. Simple by nature, the boy took my pretensions to be true, and started massaging me all over to relieve my discomfort. And, with his gentle and respectful massage of my limbs, the rest of the night passed quite agreeably. In fact, it seemed to end within moments.

'Having tricked him out of sex, at daybreak I said to myself: "This poor animal has been short-changed by me. He is as simple as a sheep and has even paid me an advance that is four times the normal fee. Now he is bound to ask for its return on the just grounds of not getting due service. This calls for somehow giving him at least a touch of intercourse, so that he has no grounds for claiming anything."

'Thinking thus as the night was ending, I commenced a play of love in return for his fee, kissing him as if with great passion. But, even after he mounted me, he continued to be full of concern for my aches and pains. "There is no need for this with me," he said kindly, whereupon, in order to humour this guileless, simple boy, I continued to wheedle him with put-on love talk.

84

"'Oh! Oh!" I sighed. "The feel of your body is pure delight. Now I truly know it. With the touch of your organ inside my place of pleasure, all my pain is gone. I don't know how, but your coming here could only have been because of good deeds in my past."

'On hearing my words, his eyes suddenly filled with tears. Obviously overcome with grief, he lost interest in making love. "Alas!" he cried, striking himself on the breast and the forehead with his hand, "It is my death. I didn't know that my body could remove a woman's pain just like medicines, incantations or precious healing stones. I am really unlucky! My dear mother died of a chronic pain, madam! Had I known this I would never have had to suffer her loss!"

'And crying, "I've been looted," he went away weeping. He was really a bull without horns in human form.

'This world is full of mindless people who always want to eat or fuck and are prepared to drop everything else. Their only pleasure is in stuffing one hole or another. They are like sheep. Without a thought, they will place their heads in the laps of those who appear trustworthy for that moment, but who are actually set on finishing them off, along with everything they have.

'Thus, one's youth must be devoted to a special, artful trade—that of relieving the unintelligent of their money in various ways. Courtesans can live only by falsehood. They need to keep away from truth, for they are destroyed by it, just as gentlewomen are by drinking.

'The splendour of courtesans is essentially untrue. It is intended to diminish other women, but the truth would destroy the courtesans themselves. For it would reveal the mansion as a poor hovel, and who would want to go there? They are, in fact, done in by reality, as merchants are by charity, teachers by humility and government officials by pity. As with the trickery of scoundrels and rogues, a courtesan's stratagems can actually evoke the admiration of others. "How smart!" they will say.

'In the old days I used to wander about this sea-girt earth. Once I was greedy and went to that home of harlotry, the city of Pataliputra. The bawds there know everything. They considered me as one with fewer skills and they loudly made fun of me. I was so ashamed that I wanted to sink into the ground.

'Because of this humiliation I went to the temple of Ganesha and began a fast without any thought for myself. In a dream, the god then asked me, repeatedly through an attendant, how long had I been fasting. "More than two months," said I, pretending that I was

87

trying to end my life. The attendant, who was omniscient, broke into a smile on hearing me. "How wonderful!" he said. "You persist in lying even during worship in a dream! Madam, I am very pleased with your unwavering adherence to untruth. You will always earn wealth through trickery and skill." This is the boon Ganesha's attendant gave me in the olden days. It shows that falsehood alone can provide for the prosperity of courtesans.

'Wealth is the chief means of life for people on this earth. It is especially so for kings intent on conquering others and also for doe-eyed courtesans. Wealth gets you knowledge and knowledge gets you wealth. The two are intertwined in this world. One who has money is honoured by everyone. He is verily the world-revered Shiva, the eloquent Brahma and the best of beings, Vishnu. And the unlucky one who does not earn money, is always a malefic planet: the heartless Rahu, the slow-moving Shani and the crooked Mangala.[11]

'A rich and well-born person is sought after as he is considered auspicious. People enjoy even his mood swings just as they do of some drunk. A wealthy man attracts them just as the shade of the sandalwood tree: they hold it in high esteem though it never bears any fruit. Even the sharpness of the affluent is well-liked, just as are their well-oiled swords. As for the poor, they get no affection, nor their dry hair any oil.[12]

'Poets and scholars, warriors and artists rise only through the patronage of the rich. They are like the planets Shukra and Budha, which come up in the sky only when Brihaspati is elevated.[13] But a learned person who is poor, even though he sells his skills like his own flesh, goes unacclaimed. And who has time for the downtrodden? Thus the meritorious are deprived and their virtues wither from within like the breasts of a widow.

'With money, men can surround themselves with scholars and be deemed learned; with warriors and be considered valiant; and with aristocrats to become famous for their lineage. Merit depends on wealth, not the other way round. That is why we sing its praises so single-mindedly.

'After all, what is better? Heaven, with its never-fading garlands and raiments, its houses of pleasure and best of women and its gay festivals? Or money? There is no question that wealth makes people blossom, like the sun makes the lotus flowers bloom. It wipes out faults and gathers friends in bright and happy celebrations. With it man becomes well-born, virtuous, helpful, respected and an exemplar to all. With it even an animal is accorded titles of excellence. What more is there to say? Money enables even the greatest of sins to be atoned for without the trouble of undergoing sacred rites, rituals and pilgrimages.

'Listen to what happened once in Varanasi, something I have heard myself. It concerns a well-known householder there, a man of standing. He was the brahmin Shridhara, a veritable god of wealth upon the earth, whose stores were as full of treasures as the ocean.

'Shridhara was like a wish-fulfilling tree for supplicants. Food fit for kings was served non-stop at his home. It was a ritual sacrifice carried out with comestibles. A thousand brahmins feeding at his mansion every day made Yudhishthira's famed exploits pale in comparison.

'Once an ascetic came to the house of this paragon. He was Jnanatma, a person of self-restraint with an other-worldly mind. Received with due honour, and respectfully invited, he was taken to see the kitchen with its vast variety of foods.

'There he beheld a corpse hanging above the foodgrains and spices, the white sacred cord around its neck. Tiny drops of blood were oozing from the dead body and, unknown to everyone, drenching the grains piled beneath. The ascetic recoiled in disgust at this hideous sight and, touching his ears in horror, he quickly slipped away unobserved.

'He returned after a year, and once more visited that house out of curiosity. The corpse was still there, he saw, but now it was fleshless and held together by its sinews. Particles of grease dripped from its hundred open veins upon the food below. He closed his eyes in utter abhorrence.

'A year later, he came again. The corpse was now a skeleton, but the grain and spices underneath were still getting soaked with the specks of fat that fell from it. Inquisitiveness brought the ascetic back the following year, when he saw that only the skull remained with its dust falling all over the grain. Six months passed, and on his next visit he noted that the kitchen was now pure and beautiful: the corpse was gone.

"'Wonderful!" the ascetic told the priests there. "This householder's plate of sins has been licked clean in a short space of time by the millions of supplicants at his great sacrificial ritual. Even the hundreds of murders and other sins committed by his forefathers and accumulated in this house have been wiped off with his charitable feasts.

"'You see," explained the ascetic, "those sins have been taken away by the people who feasted in this house. A person's sins are passed on to those who eat his food or consume his goods. Wealth is wonderful indeed. It can expiate even the grave sin of murdering a brahmin, which once had so scared the god Shiva."

'The priests extended all courtesies to the wise ascetic, who departed after inscribing with utmost respect a verse upon the rock face there. This verse is still recited by scholars and professional speakers on marvellous matters. Its meaning and mood are both profound, and I have heard it myself:

'Reverence to money,
store of good works
and home of faith;
for men the purest
place of pilgrimage
and deep meditation.
It cleanses all stains,
makes good things grow,
wards off even

unbearable curses,
and puts an end
to hordes of sins.

'After hearing this meaningful verse in praise
of wealth, I have circulated it everywhere over
the years, for it is the essence of all philosophy.
Daughter, make money as quickly as you can!
Youth alone will not help in vending the body:

'The body's vine,
the springtime's glory,
blooms but once;
the face, no more
than the full moon
of an autumn night;
and breasts burgeon only
like monsoon clouds;
youth's radiance is
just lightning's flash.

95

'You arch your brows?
But youth goes quickly
and feasts of love
where women's comely
breasts give pleasure
last no more
than a day or two.

'And the bee abuzz
around the lotus
of your lovely face,
the fawn which sports
between your breasts,
the peacock dancing
on your hips,
the royal swan
inflamed by youth
and the glory
of your midriff's slope,
will never be there long.

'Pleasure, you see, is a tethering post which youth, the elephant, will break in its determined flight. When that happens, the lovers flee, and the bosoms of their girls can only sag out of fear at being crushed in the stampede. For a woman's beautiful breasts are but a river in spate after the rain, where her lovers dance just for a moment, like maddened peacocks.

'Do not forget that youth, the friend of lovers, is ever passing. It disappears like the pretty spring creepers and the sun's warmth on the lotus pond; like autumn moonlight and the full moon's proud orb; like a simpleton's money. And when it's gone, the courtesan's glory is all of a sudden in peril.

'But it is not by youth alone that women can make money. In the woods, both the young doe and the old she-elephant can be desirable. So, my dear, put aside the conceit that your beauty is extraordinary. Splendid but proud peacocks rot in the forest, while clever crows eat of the best. The full moon can only wane, but the crooked crescent grows.

'Look, pretty-hips, your beauty is a salve for the eyes. The arch of your eyebrows surpasses the charm of Kama's bow, your visage the moon, your lips the glow of the *bimba* fruit. Yet they cannot make money for want of training, just like an elephant in rut!

'Your youth is a tree
with wondrous shade:
in which love's fever
grows sharper still.
The smile on your lips
has the glow of coral
drawn from its tendrils
in the ocean of desire.

'Your charming face and languid eyes, made up with the paste of sandalwood and curving lines of dark mascara, are like Nandana, the heavenly garden. Your waist grows even more slender, as if sad at the loss of childhood and fatigued by the weight of your breasts. But even with these looks, my beauty, you cannot acquire wealth without proper methods, just as it cannot be had simply by effort. And without wealth and the accessories that come with it, even a courtesan of charm and merit cannot attract people. It is just like the work of an able poet without sufficient means.

'Thus, pretty-eyes, a courtesan has to be extremely cunning. She must be a goddess of good luck for rich men of means, ambrosia for those bursting with cash and wine for those already besotted. For the pious, she should be a sacred conch shell and for the penniless, poison.

Like a billow on the ocean of milk of yore, she must be able to delude even the gods.'[14]

Kalavati listened to Kankali's words. She drank them in like nectar. 'Mother,' she said, 'teach me some ways to make more money.'

The Eighty Passions

The old woman began to speak about the lessons a courtesan should learn. Each was meant for trapping lustful suitors who could become like elephants in rut. 'Listen, daughter,' she said. 'Out of motherly love for you, I will say something about the various methods which you can use everywhere.

'First of all, an effort must be made to judge the suitor's state of mind. He should be accepted or rejected depending on the type of passion he manifests.

'Eight types of passions are related to the colours of certain things. These are the colours of: safflower, vermilion, saffron, lac, madder, ochre, turmeric and indigo.

'Eight are named after minerals. These are: the golden passion, that called copper, the bell-metal passion, the leaden, the ferrous, the crystal, the glassy and the stone.

'Eight passions are cosmic: those of the evening, of the moon, the rainbow and the lightning, the passions of the planets Mangala, Ketu and Rahu, and that of the sun.[1]

'Eight passions bear the names of the sense organs: those of hearing, sight, touch, taste and smell, and those born of the mind, the intellect and the ego.[2]

'Named after animals, eight passions derive from the differences between creatures.

These are the passions called the bull, the horse, the lizard, the ram, the dog, the ass, the cat and the elephant. Similarly, eight are named after birds: the parrot, the swan, the pigeon, the peacock, the sparrow, the cock, the cuckoo and the passion called the pheasant.

'Eight other kinds of passions are perceived as body parts. These are: the hair and the bone, the nail and the hand, the tooth and the foot, the beauty spot and the ear ornament.[3]

'Then there are eight proclaimed as the great passions. These are: the shadow, the ghost, the convulsive and the robber; the celestial singer, the spirit, the fury and the ghoul.

'Finally, there are the miscellaneous passions, sixteen in number. These are: the floral, the pitcher, the orange and the pomegranate; the intoxicant and the leprous; the morbid and the funeral pyre; the bee-like, the moth, the scorpion and that named fever; illusion, memory, blood and the half-moon.

'Now I will tell you, in brief, the characteristics of each passion. The safflower endures if looked after well, but will vanish within moments, if neglected. The vermilion is by nature rough but can be sustained with affection.

'The saffron is pleasant in small doses, mild and short, but when too intense, it can be painful. That named after lac will hold fast when heated up, but not when it has cooled down. The madder, on the other hand, is enjoyable both when on heat and when gone cold. The ochre's roughness keeps it steady, but excessive affection will destroy it.

'The turmeric lasts only for a moment, even when it is well tended. The indigo will, however, endure for life and, even if neglected, it will remain constant.

'Subjected to friction, cutting or heating, the golden will always be a radiant passion. But the copper shines only when rubbed hard, and in no other way. The bell-metal sullies even with affection; as for the leaden, it is always dull, from the beginning till the end.

'The passion ferrous is sharp by nature, and hard: it will not be submissive. The one named crystal is transparent, clean and constant. The glassy one is suspicious of deception and naturally fragile. The stone is enduring, but heavy, heartless and dry.

'The passion evening can be both fleeting and perpetual: it depends on the place. The lunar passion grows and dwindles, but it has a certain cooling effect which calms agony.

'The many-coloured rainbow passion is never straightforward. It can create illusions of pleasure. That called lightning springs from some change in the situation, comes on fast and fades just as suddenly. The burning-hot Mangala is ignited by abusing a woman, and that named Ketu can clearly cause calamities, leading to the likes of imprisonment and death.

'The sun passion is ever on the rise and is always uncomfortable because it is so sharp. As for the Rahu, it is immense, very coarse, and wishes to see the end of the solar passion.

'Because of its practice of giving pleasure to the ear, the passion named after it is ever-ready to hear nice things. That of the eye longs only to look at beauty and that of the tongue is greedy for myriad tastes. The passion of touch wants embracing. That named smell covets the fragrance of flowers, incense and the like.

'The passion born of the mind always seeks only the fulfilment of those desires to which it is habituated. That of the intellect is free of vice and deeply attached to a virtuous lover. And that called ego looks continuously for

106

signs of progress in achieving something it can later boast about.

'The passion bull is born of youthful pride and strength of the body. The equine is timid, but longs for intercourse and is ever-ready for it. That named after the lizard is impatient to look at women, and that of the ram wants sex in the same routine way as chewing cud.

'The canine passion turns contrary after intercourse and will also make intimacies with women public. The asinine is interested in getting satisfaction only through rough handling. The feline seeks to cuddle close. And the passion elephant does not care about obstacles or pain in its pursuit of copulation.

'The parrot is loveless inside, though outwardly it may indicate a state of enjoyment. The swan will take note of faults and skills, even in pleasure. The pigeon shows all the signs of loving during coition. The peacock is so drunk with its own beauty that it spreads itself out in advance.

'The passion sparrow seeks only one thing: union with many partners. That of the cock wants to participate in the slightest pain felt by the inamorata. The cuckoo is given to much conversation and indulges in sweet talk. The pheasant is stilled with a kiss.

'The passion hair lasts no more than seven days, and that too with difficulty. But that called bone is internalized and kept alive by unexpressed affection. The nail endures but for a month and then depletes gradually. The hand, even when it has been awakened, will not be noticed by tight-fisted temperaments. The tooth is always momentary, like the scarlet colour of the betel leaf. The one named foot can be aroused only by salutations and praise. The beauty spot is the passion of a plebeian man in intercourse with a woman of class. And the ear ornament is a devious passion, given to much ingratiating talk.

'The passion called shadow follows one everywhere, sucking one dry. That named ghost is mindless, rigid and without awareness. The convulsive is always cruel and angrily abusive. The robber will want to grab at another's clothes on a lonely road or even in public places. The singer immerses one in music, dance and suchlike. The spirit is clever at getting inside you, and will not leave, even if you try to throw it out. The fury bubbles with nonsense, but will not cause hurt. The ghoul, on the other hand, is given to dirty and violent ways, like biting and wounding the other person.

'Now, let's move on to the miscellaneous passions. The floral is candid but momentary: it accepts only praise. The pitcher will look whole even if shattered, for the pieces can be joined together. The orange is very sharp and bitter outwardly, though delectable inside. The pomegranate rises only after several children have been born to the lovers.

'The intoxicant is like a brief spell of drunkenness which is followed by a sense of embarrassment. The most disgusting passion, the leprous, is so called because it seeks satisfaction in hideous practices. The morbid wants to wound the other's tender spots. And that named funereal is created by magic rites of possession to burn up the body.

'The bee-like passion is driven only by curiosity for new tastes, flitting from one to another. The moth-like so delights in a woman's glamour that it is ready to self-destruct. The scorpion always causes pain, but this disagreeable passion is also extremely persistent. That named fever puts one off food and its great oppressiveness destroys the body's lustre.

110

'The passion named illusion displays great agitation due to loss of common sense, going round and round like a wheel. That called memory thinks of the beloved while sleeping with another woman. The passion sanguine increases with the shedding of a base person's blood in a fight. And the half-moon always celebrates sex in dreams.

'These, in brief, are the eighty well-known types of passions. Who could keep track of their number if the list were to expand? The courtesan first needs to make friends. They are as important for her welfare as the sun is for the lotus flower. It is only through such well-wishers that she can come to know potential lovers: their wealth, virtues and character, whether they are interested or not, and the ways for ensnaring their hearts. As for friends who are affectionate, very rich and inclined to lechery, she should always try to please them, even if she has to sleep with them on the quiet.

'Now, young lady, I will enumerate the kind of people among whom the best suitors are found. First, a rich man's only son, and better still if he has lost his father. Then, an official of a simple-minded king, a merchant's son who would like to emulate the fast set, or a minister who is always unwell. A doctor's son or a famous guru. A stupid but wealthy man who wishes to keep his sexual desires secret. A vegetarian, trying to dispel rumours that he is impotent. An arrogant helper of crooks or an unrestrainedly self-indulgent prince. An adulterous priest's rustic son or a professional singer who has earned a good profit. Someone who has made a quick buck or a god-fearing man of means. A fool who will blindly follow others or a scholar madly proud of his learning. And, finally, a person who is always drunk. For courtesans, all these are mobile, wish-fulfilling trees.[4]

'It is the nature of people to disdain that which is easy to get. So, when a courtesan is first approached, she should say she has no time. She should also plead a headache or some other temporary ailment, but not illness which may seem disgusting and turn people away. For the excuse should also provide for a resumption of the contact.

'The courtesan should first treat a very rich suitor with all the respect and obedience due from a wife. "You have got me in your possession," she should tell him. "I don't know whether by your wealth or by some magic art." Later, she should argue with him about his devotion to her, and even be suspicious about the love bites and scratches she herself has inflicted on his person. She should also complain at length about her keeper and should herself go to the suitor's apartment to show her keenness to be with him.

'A liaison having been formed, she should suggest to the suitor that they take a trip abroad. She should kiss him repeatedly when he is asleep and sing his praises when he is half-awake. Even in her dreams, she should mumble words about her love for him and everything connected with his name. And she should tell him to be prudent in spending money on her, so that his lust for her is never satiated.

'She should tell him, "I want to have a son by you. Without you I will die!" With such words for gaining control over the infatuated suitor, the courtesan should also proceed to get her hands on his wealth. It should be removed fast, while he is still bemused with passion. For, once that fire cools, he will become as hard as an ingot of iron. So, hold him tight between your thighs and, when his longing for sex is at its most intense, ask for everything. When a branch hangs low, you see, even a ripe mango on it will not often please someone who is already satisfied.

'Just as a lamp is kept alight with repeated drops of oil to moisten the wick, so too should the lover, who still has money, be sustained with bits of affection till he is completely cleaned out. Then, once his wealth has been taken, and his usefulness gone, drop him like a piece of sugar cane squeezed dry, in the same way as you would throw out the flowers for scenting your hair, after their freshness is gone.

'But, what if he behaves like a cat in autumn and refuses to leave your house even when asked to go? Harsh treatment is then needed. You have to hurt him where it matters the most. Hurt him with words. Get angry. Have your house-mother taunt him. Deny him your bed.

'There are also other, more crooked means like troubles foreseen through astrology and thoughts of approaching calamity. You could argue about your demands, reproach him for his lack of means and praise others for what they have given you. You could run him down with coarse language, talk of the scandal he has caused or just display indifference.

'There are other tricks too. Persist in making acerbic demands and constantly look daggers at him. Quarrel and go on a fast or go away yourself to get him out of your house.

'But, if he is so infatuated that he will not leave even after such blatant humiliation, remember that now, since his money is gone, he has become meek. The courtesan should address such a lover with arms raised and face turned away in contempt.

'"This house always used to be full of visitors and pleasure seekers of all kinds," she should say. "It is now four days since it has witnessed a festival of courtesans. What place does a eunuch with no money have in a harlot's house? Will a man, without the price of the fare in his hand, get into the ferry boat? He may be handsome, but what can a whore do with him if he has no work or money? He is a cow that neither calves nor gives milk. Of what use is it to anyone? A man with empty pockets falsely tries to please fools with loving words. He is no more than a wet nurse out of milk, who wants to bring up the baby merely by petting and kissing."

'Insulted by these words, he is bound to disappear like the frost in summer. The courtesan should then look for someone else. It could even be one who had earlier lost his money over her, but has made it again. Or another who has acquired it with effort for the first time. But he should be fit for the extraction of his riches. Having found such a lover, she should make up to him with words like, "You are my all, my heart, my very life." And, when his wealth too is gone, she should discard him like a she-serpent discards her skin, and go to another man of means. This is the sum and substance of harlotry.

'The examples I have given can be utilized in different ways during your work,' the old woman concluded. 'But you must use your own head and apply them with due thought.'

A Catch in the Morning

The moon grew dimmer rapidly,
like one whose wealth is fading fast;
the sky, perplexed by this decline,
closed its starry eyes.

Or, one might say, when the moon departed
after revelling through the night, and it was
time for the other lusty lover to arrive, the
morning twilight, like a courtesan, scattered
her starry flowers on the mantle of the sky.

And once the generous, life-giving sun had risen and the lilies had again begun to bloom, the bees started clamouring for their share of nectar, just like parasites at a pleasure party.

Kalavati was like the moonlit night bright with stars as she gazed at herself in the mirror. She wore pearls and her hair was dressed with flower garlands round which bees hummed. In her hand was a folded betel leaf, held as coquettishly as a courtesan would hold a pet parrot. Her girdle trembled and tinkled like a cooing pigeon as she climbed up to the balcony of her house on the principal highway, her hands resting on those of the barber and her newfound mother. Ready to sell her wares, she mounted the stairs as if into the arms of a lover.

Kanka the barber was already on the lookout that morning for a new suitor, fit for the pleasures of her love. Observing the activities of other courtesans now up from their beds, he said to Kalavati, 'With the appearance of the sun, the friend[1] and beloved of the day, the night clientele is going out from these women's houses.

'Look at that abbot who, with his matted hair, pretends to be like the god Shiva. Awakened suddenly by the crowing of a cock, he slips through a by-lane from Nalini's[2] house, avoiding the main road on the way back to his monastery.

'And those parasites at Bhadra's mansion this morning! They question the jail superintendent's son about his pleasures of the previous night. But actually they are busy dividing up the many goodies he had brought.

'Look at Vasantasena, who has just arrived at the front door of Anangasara, the great libertine. She is lying to him about how enjoyable her night was, even though she slept all alone! As

121

for Rama, she is weeping before her keepers as her bracelet is broken and her earrings torn by that commissioner, Matanga. Of course she will not admit her own fault in the matter.

'And look at the village official out there. He is trying to go away on the quiet, but there is an old woman behind him, trying to give him hundreds of messages for this and that.

'Here is Anangalekha, definitely setting out to have a drink with Madhava. In front of her goes the man carrying the wine jar and dragging along a sheep. And there is Shashankalekha, getting herself ready to go for a beauty treatment before meeting some soldier. But look, Mallika seems to have a problem. A date in the park with Arjuna tonight had already been fixed, but since he has not presented her the promised new Chinese garment this morning, that appointment has run into difficulty.

'Notice that procuress—she gorged herself on the mutton presented by the brahmin Indravasu last night. Now she is suffering from diarrhoea and crying for a doctor, much to the amusement of various hangers-on and loafers. Mandalagulma the doctor is making his morning rounds. He is paid with areca nuts[3] and is busy giving a fistful to Kurangika.

'Who is the woman with that bootlicker of a singer Kakshala? He smashed some utensils when denied an opportunity to perform last night, and she has got hold of his fine cloak and won't let go till he pays the price of those jars and flagons. And there is that girl Nanda with Shambhu the merchant. He came last night at his appointed time but had to sleep in an empty bed. She, on her part, has just returned from another lover's house, and is now trying to make amends by swearing false oaths.

123

'Mrinali's suitor Madan had come to her with a lot of jewellery from his father's house. Others have now arrived in search of him. Having hidden him away, she is showing these people around her own home which is quite empty. Meanwhile, Patalika is arguing with the scholar Atriratra. He has come without any worthwhile comestibles and wants to give her only a fistful of grain. "What is this for?" she says sarcastically, again and again. "Will you perform your father's last rites with this bit of rice?"

'Look at Harini's keeper, the one with the lip-licking tongue of a cat. She stole the dinner meant for Harini and Padma last night. Now that they have gone and no one else is around, she is looking about furtively and gobbling it fast.

'Then there is that pretty girl who fainted when the jealous Malaya got angry with her.

"Quickly get some jewellery and ornaments to placate her," all her friends are saying. And the guru Shambarasara, with his hair dyed black though his age is evident from his wrinkles, is off in a carriage for a religious rite at some yogi's house.

'The assembly secretary Chitivatsa is also travelling in a carriage in his worn-out suit. The nemesis of a local residential quarter and the cause of its demolition, he is well known for his unflinching cruelty.

'See, there is Kamala the officer, riding a horse. He has been gazing upwards, his sight fixed on this house. He is staring at you, Kalavati, his eyes bulging as if he were impaled. And look at that Prapancha, the Malava king's[4] envoy, with his thick gold armbands, bright crest of sandal paste and jasmine flowers. He has the lecher's sickness, evident from his decayed, cut and rejoined nose. He too is looking at you, squirming and swaying like a hypnotized snake.

'And that is the conman Shrigupta. Quick-witted and full of jokes in crooked gatherings, he is a celebrated swindler, a very Muladeva[5] in all the trickeries of this Iron Age. Look, he is busy buttering up your new house-mother, already having noticed the famous lady from afar. His hands are folded in salutation as he signals to her with glances, and strokes his chin as he smiles.

'For your mother is a veritable goddess, with a fierce mien, a vast mouth extending to the netherworld with clearly visible sharp teeth inside and a curling tongue like a flame of fire, wanting to swallow the whole world. All hail this keeper of courtesans, this accomplished lady who is withered but still brimming with plenitude.

'But there, pretty-eyes, is the son of the

merchant Shankha. The father is loaded with money. Greedy and the very image of sin, he is a dealer in precious goods. The son, Panka, is a mere child, as simple as a fawn. Attracted by the loafers coming out from the house next door, he is gazing at you like a sparrow hopping about on a heap of straw. He has fat cheeks, long hair, gold earrings hanging down to his shoulders and the mind of a lamb. He is indeed a treasure that fate has sent for you.'

Kankali had been thinking as she listened to Kanka's descriptions. She looked at the merchant's son and, satisfied that he would provide a desirable profit, smiled and said: 'His neck is spotted with drops of betel-juice stains. He turns it to look this way and that as he staggers about in his red shoes. He is an effortless catch for a courtesan to make money. If such a simple lad turns up on his own it is only because of her good deeds in a previous birth.'

'Kalavati,' she continued, 'he has set his eyes on your face! It seems circumstance has brought this young beast to your temple as a victim for the sacrifice of love. Kanka, go to him quickly. His people will use you as the go-between.'

Thus instructed by Kankali, the barber descended from the balcony and cheerfully went out.

Meeting the Lover

Spring came softly, bright with flowers,
glorious, by vines caressed,
awakening to life, afresh,
Kama, springing in the mind.

The sun moved north, towards the quarter of
the god of wealth,[1] as if acknowledging that
on him depended the richness of a lover's
pleasure. Breezes blew from the south, wafting
as though the sighs of slender vines laden with

creamy flowers, like girls in white separated from their lovers. Kama, burnt down by the angry Shiva in ancient times, was resurrected by the king of the seasons.[2]

The new season filled the forests with glory. Echoing the cuckoo's song and the bumblebee's hum, the air became heady with the scent of honey, like a courtesan drunk on wine. Plants sprouted myriads of new buds in the intoxicating embrace of spring. The hibiscus turned scarlet, as if with jealousy at this fresh effusion of love. It seemed that the goddess of the woods had cast aside the old and worn-out winter, spurned its cool but deep passion, and cuddled up to spring, her chosen boy. In effect, age is no bar once women decide to do something.

The barber turned go-between, made several trips back and forth. At first Kalavati avoided making a decision on whether to accept the lad or not. Eventually she agreed in view of the profit and commenced her toilet for the evening's rendezvous.

The elegance of Kalavati's make-up had never been so delightful. An angled leaf design in musk was etched on her temple, a beauty spot of camphor was marked on her forehead near the curling hair and her body was tinted with golden saffron. A girdle encircled her hips. 'I am used to mature lovers,' she murmured bashfully, 'perhaps I am not suitable for a boy.' But her lissom body, her breasts and her gaze, all were captivating as she readied herself for love.

Meanwhile, the merchant's son had entered the courtesan's house. Heavy rings of gold strung with pearls dangled, doubtless painfully, from his ears. Four golden amulets hung from the ornament round his neck. On his ankles glittered a pair of silver anklets studded with little globes of lapis lazuli. His mother had placed some mustard seeds in his hair for good luck. He was surrounded by local residents intent on making some profit.

He came in fiddling with the end of a long sash which kept slipping off his shoulder, and sucking in through his teeth as his mouth had been scalded by the excessive lime paste in the betel leaf he had chewed. He gazed at Kalavati in awe. Reflected in a mirror placed towards the east, she appeared like a moonlit night and the stars in her necklace seemed to smile down on her bosom. 'This child is fit only for petting,' they seemed to say. 'How will he fare in love's battle?'

He was preceded by seven well-known parasites. They were like the seven clever priests who ordained one at a religious ceremony held for expending one's capital. These bumblebees hovering around our young lotus of love were: a junior officer named Kshinasara; Kamalakara, a bureaucrat; the drama teacher Rechaka; the goldsmith Kshunnapani; Simhagupta the astrologer; a doctor's son, Tikta; and Kutilaka, a poet.

They had already instructed the boy on decorum while they waited outside the house. After coming in, he sat down boldly by the girl's side like a mature man. Covering half his nose with his sash, he then began to repeat the disagreeable, superior-sounding jokes he had learnt, just like a trained parrot.

Kankali entered. Taking a more elevated seat, she began to propitiate the parasites with deceitful words of praise. 'This handsome lad is blessed to have your company,' she told them. 'He has earned your acquaintance only as a result of good deeds in his past lives. Even though he is just a child, we have the highest respect for this lover. For, it is only the newly risen sun which makes a lily bloom.'

While they spat betel juice and covered the floor with pink spots, Kankali won the parasites over with such eulogies. Kalavati's dark-skinned nurse, Vetalika, was happy at the opportunity to distribute betel leaf again. 'This is a very intimate assembly of betel lovers,' she said with some emotion. 'We do not collect countless numbers like other courtesans.'

'The first who should be honoured is Kanka,' she continued. 'He is generous and looks like a god. At his request, even the hard-to-get Kalavati becomes approachable. Also esteemed is the son-in-law, whom we are honouring with our girl. No less deserving of respect is Kamala, the conch-shell merchant.

'Here is the great ritualist Shakti who performed the last rites for Kalavati's father. He returned just yesterday for a sacred feast. And this is the landlord's son Kapila, also called Kalasha. Our bartender this evening is Kalpapala, who shares the same guru with Kalavati.

'That is Mridangodara, the husband of Kalavati's sister. Kalaha is her maternal uncle and Bindusara her natural brother. And that is the nurse of Kalavati's adopted son, Kalayusha. Her name too is Kalavati, and there is her husband, Rugnachandra.

'This is Kamba, the son of Bhagavata. He is an expert in Bharata's science of drama. And that is the minister's friend, the singer Swaradasa. Also present are Nigila the chef, Karpara the potter, Baka the umbrella bearer and Khanjana the coachman.

'There is the brahmin Ratisharma, who propitiates the planets for courtesans, the garden keeper Karala and the boatman Kilavarta. Near them are Kanda, the guard of the park, Mukula the florist, Varmadatta the tanner and Marachhidra the courier.

The sweeper Gharghara is shouting outside and with her are Chandarava the musician and Praharika the storekeeper. All these people have to be served the betel leaf. But to Kalavati's girlfriend Shambaramala and her guru Dambhabhuti, it needs to be sent first thing in the morning.'

Thereafter, Vetalika sent away with all respect the various people who had been entering and leaving the house. Intent on getting some betel leaf, they were now making eyes at each other after drinking much liquor.

Meanwhile, the night was passing like incense smoke, with the parasites getting drunk and bragging incoherently. 'I am the king's right hand during battle!' cried one. 'The kingdom lives within my pen,' proclaimed another. 'The science of dramaturgy depends on me,' shouted the third. 'The rich man's treasure comes out of my balance,' asserted the next. They were all inebriated as they argued. 'I can divine the state of all things through my calculations.' 'I alone could cure King Bhoja.'[3] 'Many kings have honoured me for my poems.'

Eventually, after a show of farewell and an offer of betel leaf, Kalavati got them all to leave, and they departed making estimates of the money she would be making. Her pretty face still lit up with a smile at their jokes, and the doe-eyed girl then took the intoxicated boy to her bed. A canopy stretched above it. Beneath was spread a spotless sheet of Chinese cloth with pillows as white as a swan's wing.

As with that child
she dallied and sported,
dark smoke, as of incense,

rose up from the lamps;
was it a bee swarm
drawn to their fragrance,
or were the lamp flames
flickering with shame?

The Goal Attained

The stars were drowsy,
it was as if
the toil of love
with the silvery moon
had made the night languid,
as it turned pale
and wet with drops
of morning dew.

It was morning. The courtesan's eyes were red

with having kept awake all night. She went to Kankali who was ready with questions about the nocturnal pleasures. 'Listen, mother,' Kalavati told her, 'in age he may be a child, but it is quite clear that he has grown before his time. For one so young, he is as sharp as a peppercorn.

'Gently taken by my servant girl to a raised bed, that cunning boy lay there with his body motionless for a while, pretending to be asleep. I embraced him with the impulsive curiosity which comes easily to women and then, within moments of the first intercourse, he suddenly turned totally inert.

'Thinking that the narcotic betel nut had affected him, I put my hand on his breast. I wet it with cold water, hoping that the shock of drowning in some deluge would bring him back to his senses. And then he was wide awake. He had already tasted the pleasure, and now he was all over me like a sparrow and, with numberless mountings, wore me out to exhaustion.

'His face may be that of a boy's but he is much more than a young man. It was rash of me to wake him up. Alas, in doing so, I took a flaming piece of coal in my own hand. I refrained from giving him love bites out of pity that he was a child who would start weeping. But look at my lips which he bit like a parrot and scarred so many times. And at my breasts, which he so pressed down with his repeated clambering and hugs that for a moment they refused to regain their shape, as if ashamed of their union with an infant. He has left marks even on the private parts of my body! How will I conceal them when I am with shrewd and experienced men?'

The courtesan had been affected by her all-night vigil. For a moment she looked bashful, her gaze lowered to the ground. Kankali smiled as she replied, her big teeth sticking out as if to crush the parasites' expectations from the affair. 'You simpleton,' she said, 'the children of businessmen are like this, sharp as nails. Their boldness is also nurtured by the loafers and goons they associate with in the market.

'This boy has definitely got hold of some money from his father's house. Such audacity can never come out of an empty pocket. Even a mouse jumps about no end when there are foodgrains in its burrow. An elephant with a dried-up trunk can only go to sleep.

'So, I am going to fix up this merchant's son as the source of your livelihood. But first the hive must be rid of the bees, that is, I must arrange to get his hangers-on out of here. Every limb of ours is a rich, marketable treasure house. Why should these bastards eat off it?'

Saying this, Kankali hastened to the bedroom. She talked to the boy, one on one, in an intimate manner. 'Son,' she said, 'did the whole night pass well with that pretty girl? You deserve to be arrested by us, for you have stolen Kalavati's heart. She is lost in thought, sighing and yawning, trembling and stumbling, even while you are here. What will she do when you are gone?

'Kalavati has gone through a sea of young men. The southern ruler Bhoja[1] has sought her through his envoys. But she is totally attached to you. If this union were not ordained by fate from your previous lives, why would I cherish the hope that you will perform the filial last rites when I die?

'But I can think of one obstacle to your union, and that makes me afraid. It is this bunch of parasites who surround you like a net of thorns. These rogues live off the money of others. They never waste any of their own. Having eaten and drunk off you, they will hand you over to your father's custody. So, if you stay well-hidden here, even for a day, this horde of crooks will lose hope and scatter.'

Youth had made the merchant's son guileless. 'Mother,' he replied, 'what you say so lovingly is quite true. Tied within this cloth is something from my father's store. Take it for your daughter's toilet and other expenses.' Then, giving her a large sum of his father's money, he went off through the secret passage she showed him into a large cellar underneath the house.

The overjoyed Kankali promptly hid the money. Pulling a long face of false sorrow, she approached the parasites who were now beginning to get noisy. 'We had treated you as our natural lifelong friends,' she said to them. 'Our loving hospitality has been to your satisfaction. Was it then proper for you gentlemen to behave so disgracefully? Was it a merchant's son whom you brought last night to this house full of gems and jewellery or was it a dangerous brigand? Even if you were bent on making fun of us at the behest of other courtesans, how could you dare to commit a sin as great as murdering a woman?'

'This morning,' she continued, 'when Kalavati had fallen asleep for a moment, that lecher took her pair of armbands along with her necklace and disappeared. We hear that courtesans are being murdered for their jewellery in every town. It is only by her personal god's grace that Kalavati escaped alive.

'If this matter is taken to the court,' she cried, 'on whose head will the blame fall? Which courtesan will stand bail for the likes of you?' And with these words, Kankali ran out on to the highway as if no longer able to tolerate a fierce quarrel within the house, screaming loudly at the passers-by.

'Look, O people!' she raved. 'Look at the evil times upon us—rich and loving friends now entertain the sin of murdering women. Who knows what virtue is? Who can tell one's breeding by looking at the hand? Crooks say one thing and do another. It is just impossible to comprehend.'

The parasites turned pale with fear. Dispirited and at a loss for words, they quickly fled through various lanes to meet at a distance. There they consulted each other for a long time. Beset by problems, deprived of their pleasures and terrified of false charges, they began to disperse: all the trouble they had taken had turned out to be fruitless.

'We never saw that merchant's boy leave,' said the junior officer. 'We have been tricked

146

by Kankali, just as is done with loaded dice.'
'Look,' observed the bureaucrat after some
thought, 'it is concealment of commercial
capital by the suppression of a document. That
is what the madam has done to us.'

'It was a planned performance,' the drama
teacher proclaimed. 'But her role was in an act
which is over. Now it is we who are dancing,
isn't it?' But the goldsmith was angry. 'I know
that Kankali,' he cried. 'She is like a fraudulent
balance with hundreds of calibrations. This is
all her doing.'

'Just as the sun is pulled out of the ram's sign
in the course of time,'[2] explained the astrologer
with an ovine pun, 'so has Kankali taken the
merchant away from his friends and a feast of
the ram's flesh.' 'Well, we drank a lot of wine,'
the doctor remarked, 'so she is now treating
us. Teetotalism is her prescription for pyrexia.'
'Anyway,' sighed the poet who was off colour,

'our rules and rhythms have been upset and our attainment of happiness set at naught. This is something beyond any comparison.'

The parasites were angry and distressed, ashamed as well as amazed. Talking amongst themselves, they departed like bees driven out of a flower garden. As for Kankali, she spent a problem-free night quietly by herself, enjoying the festive fare as she pleased. She also had another stratagem in mind. Having thought it over, the next morning she passed by the great store in the market and saw for herself the enormous riches of the young man's progenitor, the merchant.

Even though he had already accumulated great wealth and profit, the merchant's rapacity was such that the thought of his son stealing his gold troubled him no end. He sat on a high cushioned seat, with a box of documents worth three million in his hand. He appeared blind to his supplicants, for his eyes were closed as he refused to look at their faces. To their requests for reduction of interest or release of goods on pledge, he turned a deaf ear. As for responding to questions about even very small discounts, he was completely mute.

He had a large, unkempt knotted beard, and wore a hideous cap with hair-oil stains, half of it gnawed away by mice. A worn-out woollen cloak hung over his thick tunic, its tail fluttering beneath. The lower garment of a deep, smoky-red material was torn and loose, leaving a thigh and a knee bare.

The merchant was merciless, unresponsive even to the cries of a pet cat which was tied up and hungry. He was angry and about to strike the little girl who had come from his own home to ask for money for the daily expenses when Kankali saw him.

Her finger resting on one side of her nose,

she took stock of him from a distance. 'So this is the famous merchant,' she said to herself. Then, approaching him slowly when the others had gone and the coast seemed clear, she said, 'Master of the store, there is something I have to tell you in private. Last evening, some greedy parasites got hold of your son, who is as simple-minded as a fawn, and looted him of his ornaments and clothes. I saw this, and feeling sorry for that handsome lad, I brought him to my own house. But then, I do not know how, within moments he captivated my daughter.'

'She most lovingly presented him with a fine dress and ornaments,' Kankali continued. 'After he had bathed, she served him all kinds of delicacies fit for a king. Her devotion to him is such as though he were Kama himself. To her, he seems as close and precious as the necklace round her throat. He has so many merits—a family of distinction, good character and such admirable looks. Together with all the wealth you have earned by working for princes and ministers, you also have a treasure of a son who has now become my daughter's husband by their association in a previous birth.

'My young Kalavati is madly in love and fortunate to have found someone more than suitable. I now place her in your hands, together with her personal wealth and house. Everything is certified and sealed. You must guard all she has, especially when I leave on pilgrimage after some time. But today, sir, you must come to our house, for the love of your son and at the request of your daughter-in-law, to eat a little something at the feast held to bless them.'

With tears in her eyes, Kankali then fell at the merchant's feet. The man had a heart of stone, but he was pleased, particularly to get word of his son. 'My good lady,' he replied, 'all this is indeed very welcome news. But I cannot agree to your leaving by yourself, so let us go together. Moreover, it is my rule never to eat another's food. So how can I dine at your house? I will come only if you let me pay for my dinner.' Saying this he placed a silver *rupaka* coin and a half in Kankali's palm, and she departed with a smile on her face.

Later, when he came for the feast, the merchant saw his son enjoying himself with his inamorata. That the lavish arrangements had cost him nothing allayed his cares and worries, making him quite well disposed. Having eaten his fill of delicacies flavoured with cardamom and camphor, and drunk amply of wine, the miser went up to Kankali. 'I will always give you people appropriate funds for all your daily expenditure,' he told her. 'But such heavy expenses should not be incurred again.'

After that visit, the merchant went home, building castles in the air. Tempting them with profit is indeed the best way to fool greedy minds. On the following day, Kalavati sent her personal maid to the crook, to collect the promised money for their daily expenditure and also to assess his intentions. The servant returned after a long time with an earthen cup and some grains of asafoetida wrapped in birch bark. Kalavati was all smiles as she snapped her fingers at her mistress. 'Your father-in-law has sent this vast and valuable quantity of eatables,' said the maid. 'Get up, invite your friends and distribute it.'

'He gave me this ounce of oil,' she continued, 'and two of this powdered salt. Knitting his brows, he said: "Here is the oil. Here is the salt. Here are two cowries[3] for the greens. Which lover gives thousands for a courtesan's daily expenses?"' Then, displaying what had been sent, she spat upon it several times and threw it away, cursing her own eyes for having been sullied by looking at the donor's face.

On the following day, Kankali thought of another scheme to trick the merchant painlessly. Explaining it in private to Kalavati, she went out to make the arrangements.

She had two caskets made of the identical colour, size and seals. One she filled with jewellery and the other with bits of stone. Covering each with a thick pad of cotton, she hid them in her cloak and went to the merchant's store.

'The propitious time for my journey on pilgrimage to Varanasi has arrived,' she told the merchant. 'Once I leave, I may not see you again. Here is a casket with all our gem-studded jewellery. It is the wealth of your son

154

and his wife. You, sir, must always guard it as if it were your life.'

Having shown him all its contents and resealing the jewel casket, she placed it before him. 'Comrade,' she then said, teasing him, 'I hardly need a hundred thousand for my travel expenses. But you should at least give me enough to cover what is required for food at the temples on the way.' And, as she joked and bantered, Kankali exchanged the two caskets, swiftly collected a hundred thousand in cash and returned home.

Seeing the keeper back, Kalavati knew that the task had been accomplished. She then took the son of Shankha the merchant to a quiet place in her mansion. 'I have given you my heart,' she told him. 'No force can get it back to me. But you are rich and I am concerned that you will go and get married.'

'Having a wife,' she added, 'may be pleasant

for a while, but for life it cannot be worse. Even so, deluded and unthinking men are eager for matrimony. What pleasure can wives give? Their youth degenerates with repeated childbirth. Their passion declines. They are devoid of courtesans' graces and have no interest in the delights of conversation. All they are good at is starting quarrels.

'Courtesans, on the other hand, are born to please men. They have every grace for this. They are fragrant, flirtatious and devoted to carnal pleasure. Who will not love an ever-smiling courtesan? So, for my assurance, give me a power of attorney to your wealth. That will help me to keep you, like a rutting elephant is kept by the goad.'

The merchant's son wrote out a long credit note in the name of Vikrama Shakti, the queen's nephew. The next morning Kankali herself visited him in the bedroom. 'Your youth is blooming,' she said, pulling a long face, 'but my daughter's you have practically finished off. The youth of women fades suddenly, unbeknown to others. That of men is long-lasting by nature, like tall trees. The woman, who was a child yesterday and today is a damsel, will become a crone tomorrow.'

'It is now two days over a month since Kalavati has had her period,' Kankali continued. 'She is very worried that she may have become pregnant. Childbirth is a curse for the beauty of a young woman. It is a shower of frost upon the lily which is her body, a fierce crime against her breasts. They droop, as if in shame, after youth falls prey to bearing children. As for courtesans, no one cares a straw for them then. Men can lead an easy life in old age through knowledge. But a courtesan must go around begging once her youth is gone. This being the case, you, who are so wise, should write out a letter of authority giving Kalavati all the property after your father is no more.'

Inspired by what the old bawd had said, the merchant's son happily passed his inheritance in favour of Kalavati. Kankali's deference to him slackened thereafter. Two or three days later, on a signal from her, Kanka the barber spoke aloud to Kalavati within the boy's hearing.

'For whom are you so lovelorn, Kalavati?' said the barber. 'For whom are you keeping these fasts? The knight's son Ranavilasa has been asking for you. The temple treasurer Makaragupta counts himself blessed even by your brusque replies to his many requests for a meeting. The great minister Satyaratha has today sent a pair of festive garments for you, yet you show him no favours. Prince Sahasaraja saw you at the festival, and was so besotted that he has abandoned his concubine Vasavasena.'

'You simpleton!' the barber cried. 'If you while away this time when you are young with just one patron you happen to like, who will give you any money when it is over? Girls who have neglected making money in their youth because of love, now go about with ash-besmeared bodies or in the rags of a nun.

'In love play, you are a queen, with your splendid rear for a throne, your breasts golden pitchers and your smile the royal parasol. Indeed, you should be enjoyed by just one man, but he should be a king. Do not, my pretty, think that because you took a man's money, you have to be good to him even when his wealth is gone. What you ate yesterday is not going to sustain you today.

'A slave is a slave only till the master has something in hand. Once his wealth depletes, she should be as difficult for him to reach as heaven itself. It is a foolish man who thinks "I gave her money yesterday. So, how can I leave today?" For, courtesans are available only for the moment when the cash is gifted.'

Kanka's words to Kalavati were arrows that pierced the merchant's son. For a moment he was stunned as he stared at the ground in embarrassment. Thereafter, the girl started making all kinds of excuses to keep Shankha's offspring out of her bed. 'Today I am observing a fast for the mother goddess as I had a bad dream. Tonight it is the holy sixth and there is a wake at the royal palace to which I have to go. Today is the hair-cutting ceremony of my friend's son Mriganka Datta.' Under such pretexts, she also started going to the houses of other suitors.

One morning Kankali rushed up to Shankha's son, trembling and shaking, as if in great fear. 'Get up, son!' she told him. 'Be quick. Cover your head and flee. A murder has been committed here. It is one of the two rivals who were quarrelling about us. Kalavati has already gone to a friend's house. You are a good person, but a rich merchant's son. The city chief is very difficult and the king runs after the very scent of lucre. So, leave your quilted cloak and take a dust bag from the grindstone on your back. Who knows what will happen if someone were to recognize you on the way.'

Kankali's words were just a pack of lies to get rid of this thorn in her side. But Panka did all that she told him, and fled from the mansion through the back lane.

A vine's new shoots are full of colour at first. Then the colour fades and finally disappears. The courtesan is a vine, and her love is like the changing colour of a new shoot. In it is seen her real disposition.

Kankali had been appointed the courtesan's keeper. With her intelligence and cooperation,

Kalavati acquired all that the merchant had and became extremely affluent. This is how wicked and cunning madams cheat customers of love in so many ways. These fawns see deer traps in the forest every day, but even then, they let themselves get ensnared. Kalavati got herself a mother by contract in good time. And it is with that very name of *Samaya Mātrikā*[4] that Kshemendra has composed this work.

Epilogue

She is arrayed in ornaments and charming inflections. She is elegant and delightful, a domicile for distinction, a pleasure at leisure. She derives substance even from fools. She can be invoked to enjoy the newest tastes and the most marvellous delineations. Like the muse of a good poet, an accomplished and mature courtesan steals the hearts of all.

In the five and twentieth year,
on the Pausha month's first day
when the moon begins to wax,
this feast of smiles was put together
to guard the wealth of gentlemen.

An old, afflicted forest woman
tells the travellers passing by:
'Here in mountain burrows sleep
hordes of fearsome hooded serpents;
there live rutting elephant herds;
that cave is home to lions; and
in the jungle bush, beware,
are bandit girls to catch you.'

Epilogue

Brave, compassionate to the troubled,
adorned by conduct's purity,
the sword his one companion
in conquering the enemy:
in that King Ananta's reign
over a great and growing realm,
Kshemendra this work created—
of well-said verses, capable
of keeping good people safe.

Notes

Introduction

1. Listed as serial numbers 4, 5, 6, 8, and 10 of Appendix A.
2. Ibid., number 18.
3. *Brihatkathāmanjari*, epilogue, vv. 1, 3, 5.
4. Ibid., v. 7.
5. Ibid., v. 38.
6. *Avadānakalpalatā*, 108, 12, 13, epilogue.
7. *Auchitya Vichāra Charchā*.
8. *Kavikanthābharaṇa*.

9. Appendix A.

10. Ibid., serial numbers 11, 12, 13, 14, 15 and 16. The authorship of the last mentioned is disputed.

11. Ibid., serial numbers 17 and 18.

12. *Rājataraṅgiṇi*, trans. R.S. Pandit (New Delhi: Sahitya Akademi, 1986), 1.13. Hereafter referred to as *RT*.

13. A.K. Warder, *Indian Kavya Literature*, vol. 6 (Delhi: Motilal Banarsidass, 1992).

14. Introduction to S.C. Ray's *Early History and Culture of Kashmir* (Delhi: Munshiram Manoharlal, 1970).

15. Warder, *Indian Kavya Literature*.

16. Appendix B.

17. *Samaya Mātrikā* 1.91; Ray, *Early History and Culture of Kashmir*; and Warder, *Indian Kavya Literature*.

18. K.M. Panikkar in the introduction to Ray's *Early History and Culture of Kashmir*.

19. *Kṣemendra Laghu Kāvya Saṃgraha* (Minor Works of Kṣemendra), ed. E.V.V. Raghavacharya and D.G. Padhye, General Editor Aryendra

Sharma (Hyderabad: Osmania University, 1961); and *Samaya Mātrikā*, ed. R. Tripathi (Varanasi: Chowkhamba Vidyabhawan, 1967).

20. Warder, *Indian Kavya Literature*; Ray, *Early History and Culture of Kashmir*; *RT*; B. Chaturvedi, *Kshemendra* (New Delhi: Sahitya Akademi, 1983); Surya Kanta, *Kṣemendra Studies* (Pune, 1954); and U. Chakraborty, *Kṣemendra* (Delhi: Indian Books Centre, 1991).

A Worrying Question

1. The site is identified with present-day Srinagar. See Appendix B for this and other names of places, especially for the following chapter.
2. In mythology, the great god Shiva incinerated Kama, the god of love, with a fiery gaze when the latter attempted to distract him during his meditation.

The Story of a Life

1. An honorific title indicating persons of distinction.
2. Kamboja and Trigarta are names of areas and people in the north-west of the South Asian subcontinent; Gauda, Anga and Vanga in the east; and Turushka indicates Turkish people.

Kankali

1. The well-known trinity of the Hindu pantheon, Brahma, Vishnu and Shiva are, respectively, the gods of creation, preservation and dissolution. Brahma, envisioned with four faces is also the source of the four Vedas. Among Vishnu's many attributes is the lordship of *maya* or worldly delusion. Shiva, one of whose epithets is Bhairava, is also a fierce protector. The references here are satirical.
2. The point of the satirical comment is that oil and wool would have then been more plentiful and easier to obtain.

3. A reference to the mythology of Vishnu's incarnations. As the divine tortoise, he supported Mount Mandara which was used as the churning stick when the gods and the demons churned the ocean to gain its treasures. As the enchantress Mohini, he then distracted the demons from using the nectar of immortality yielded by the ocean.

   Vishnu is also pictured as asleep on a serpent bed in the ocean, reclining on his consort Shri, or Lakshmi. In his incarnation as the celestial boar, he rescued the earth by hauling it up from the ocean's depths. As the dwarf incarnation, he begged for three steps' worth of land from the demon Bali, and assumed a colossal form to take his entire kingdom. He is also considered the best of beings and without any attributes.

4. Shambhu is an epithet of the great god Shiva. He is usually portrayed with a crescent moon on his brow. Garbed as an ascetic and sometimes riding on a bull, he is often surrounded by naked ascetic attendants. In another portrayal, he and

his consort are fused in a single body, half-woman and half-man. Here, all this is satirical as with Brahma and Vishnu in the preceding paragraphs.

5. The reference is to a literary tradition that in the season of spring if a pretty girl touches an ashoka tree with her foot, it will begin to flower; it also refers to the bees which sip the flowers' nectar like rogues taking advantage of a distraught lover.

6. Mara is another name for Kama, though more current in Buddhist mythology. He tried to disturb Shiva's meditation but was incinerated by the great god. See note 2 on p. 169. The Kshemendra text makes double use of the word *guṇa* which means both quality and bowstring.

7. In another legend, Indra, the king of heaven, was punished for committing adultery and cursed to have such marks all over his body.

8. See note 3 above. The churning of the ocean yielded many treasures apart from the nectar of immortality. These included the divine elephant and horse, the wish-fulfilling tree and the spirit

of wine. But the reference here is dismissive. The churning also produced a terrible poison which Shiva swallowed, to prevent it from destroying the world.

9. Well-known instances of human folly from the epics *Rāmāyaṇa and Mahābhārata*.

10. Another legend about how the nectar of immortality found its way to the gods. Garuda is the divine mount of Vishnu. Nagas were denizens of the netherworld.

11. In traditional Indian astrology some planets are classified as fierce and sometimes malefic. These include Shani, or Saturn; Mangala, or Mars; and Rahu, conceptualized as a 'shadow planet' and referred to as the Dragon's Head. For the laudatory references in the preceding sentence, see note 1 above.

12. Kshemendra makes double use here of the word *sneha*, meaning both affection and oil.

13. It was believed that the appearance in the sky of the planets Shukra (Venus) and Budha (Mercury), followed that of Brihaspati (Jupiter).

14. The references in this paragraph are to some of the treasures yielded by the ocean of milk when it was churned. See note 8 above.

The Eighty Passions

1. All fierce planets. See note 11 on p. 173. Ketu, another 'shadow planet', is referred to as the Dragon's Tail.
2. These three are also considered sensory instruments in traditional Indian psychology.
3. The inclusion of the last two in this list is explicable only perhaps in terms of their common use by people at the time.
4. The wish-fulfilling tree was one of the treasures obtained from the churning of the ocean. See note 8 on p. 172. The adjective 'mobile' added here appears to be a sarcastic comment.

A Catch in the Morning

1. A double use has been made here of the word

mitra, which is another name of the sun god and also means a friend.

2. This and other women's names in subsequent paragraphs refer to various courtesans whose activities are described therein.

3. The nut commonly chewed with the betel leaf. It was obviously an imported luxury in Kashmir and here is used for payment in kind.

4. See note 3 of the next chapter on p. 176.

5. Known in Sanskrit literature as the exponent of the science of theft.

Meeting the Lover

1. The guardian of the northern quarter in Hindu mythology is Kubera, the god of wealth.

2. See note 2 on p. 169. Vasanta, the personification of spring, is the vanguard and comrade of Kama. His arrival as a prelude to Kama's attempted distraction of the great god Shiva is most famously described in the *Kumārasambhava* of Kalidasa.

3. The well-known ruler of Dhara in western India, who reigned c. 1018–1055 CE, was also famous as a scholar and patron of literature. The reference to 'the Malava king' on p. 125 is probably also to him.

The Goal Attained

1. See note 3 of the previous chapter above.
2. One of the signs of the zodiac.
3. A small shell once used as the lowest unit of currency.
4. See the Introduction for a literal translation of this term.

Epilogue

1. The contemporary king of Kashmir during the author's time. See the Introduction.

Appendix A:
Kshemendra's Works

WORKS LOCATED, EDITED AND PRINTED

Abridgements

1. *Brihatkathāmanjari* (Kavyamala, N.S. Press, Mumbai, 1901)
2. *Bhāratamanjari* (Kavyamala 18, N.S. Press, Mumbai, 1903)

3. *Rāmāyaṇamanjari* (Kavyamala 83, N.S. Press, Mumbai, 1903)

Poetics

4. *Suvrittatilaka* (Kavyamala 2, N.S. Press, Mumbai, 1886)
5. *Kavikanthābharaṇa* (Motilal Banarsidass, Varanasi, 1967)
6. *Auchitya Vichāra Charchā* (Chowkhamba Vidyabhawan, Varanasi, 1992)

Satires

7. *Kalāvilāsa* (Kavyamala 1, N.S. Press, Mumbai, 1886)
8. *Samaya Mātrikā* (Kavyamala 10, N.S. Press, Mumbai, 1888)
9. *Deśopadeśa* (Kashmir Sanskrit Series 40, Srinagar, 1923)
10. *Narmamālā* (Kashmir Sanskrit Series 40, Srinagar, 1923)

Didactic Works

11. *Lokaprakāśa* (Kashmir Sanskrit Series 75, Srinagar, 1947)
12. *Nītikalpataru* (BORI, Pune, 1956)
13. *Chaturvargasaṃgraha* (in *Minor Works of Kṣemendra*, Osmania University, Hyderabad, 1961)
14. *Chārucharyā* (as in 13)
15. *Darpadalana* (as in 13)
16. *Sevyasevakopadeśa* (as in 13)

Others

17. *Avadānakalpalatā* (Bibliotheca Indica 1.2, Kolkata, 1940)
18. *Daśavatāracharita* (Munshiram Manoharlal, Delhi, 1983)

Works Known Only through Citations

1. *Amritataranga*
2. *Avsarasāra*

3. *Lāvaṇyavatī*
4. *Padyakādambarī*
5. *Vinayavalli*
6. *Muktāvali*
7. *Pavana Panchāśikā*
8. *Munimata Mīmāṃsā*
9. *Śaśivaṃśa*
10. *Lalitaratnamālā*
11. *Kanakajānaki*
12. *Chitrabhārata*
13. *Nitimālā*
14. *Kavikarṇikā*
15. *Vātsyāyana Sūtra Sāra*
16. *Nṛpāvali*

Of the titles in this list of unlocated works, the possible subject matter of 4, 15 and 16 is mentioned in the Introduction. From the comments of some scholars cited there, it would appear that 1, 2 and 7 were descriptive poems; 6, 8 and 14, works on poetics; 5 and 13, didactic works on conduct; 11 and 12, plays based on incidents in the *Rāmāyaṇa* and the *Mahābhārata* respectively; 10 derived from Harsha's play *Ratnāvali* of c. seventh century CE; and 9 a poetic account of the lunar race of kings. These must naturally remain conjectures till the actual texts of these works come to light.

Appendix B:
Place Names

Identified names of places in the order of their appearance in the text:

1. Pravarapura. The location corresponds with present-day Srinagar. It was founded by the sixth-century king Pravarasena and is mentioned by Kalhana (*RT* 3.358).
2. Parihasapura. It is identified with *pargana* Paraspor, south-west of Shadipur. It was built as the new capital by the eighth-century king

Lalitaditya, but the seat of government was later shifted by his successor.

3. Shankarapura. It is identified with the village Patan on the Srinagar–Baramulla road, about seven miles west of Parihasapura. Kalhana describes it as a trading town (*RT* 5.162).

4. Pratapapura. Identified with the village Tapar on the Srinagar–Baramulla road.

5. Sureshvari. It was a hill shrine on the bank of the Shatadhara Spring, north-east of Pravarapura.

6. Vijayeshvara. It is identified with Vijabror.

7. Avantipura. Located near the village Vantipor on the river Jhelum, it has old temple ruins. It was founded in the ninth century by King Avantivarman and is mentioned by Kalhana (*RT* 7.1366).

8. Krityashrama. It was a monastery five miles west of Huskapura, the site of the village Uskar near Baramulla.

9. Shurapura. It is identified with the village Hurapor near the stream Rembyar on the route leading to the Pir Panjal Pass.

10. Panchala. It is actually mentioned in the text
    (2.92) as Pachaladhara Matha, a hospice or
    monastery located about four to five miles north
    of the Pir Panjal Pass.

Scholars mentioned in the Introduction have based
these findings chiefly on the work of Sir Aurel Stein
indicated in the footnotes to his translation of the
Rājataraṅgiṇi, Chronicle of the Kings of Kashmir,
2 vols (London: Constable & Co., 1900).

ALSO IN PENGUIN CLASSICS

Kama Sutra
Vatsyayana

Translated by A.N.D. Haksar

'A fine new translation'—*Guardian*

'A clear and elegant new translation'
—*New York Times*

Treating pleasure as an art, *Kama Sutra* is a handbook covering every aspect of love and relationships. This new edition highlights the work's historical importance as a sophisticated guide to living well. Conveying all the original flavour and feel of this elegant, intimate and hugely enjoyable work, Haksar's clear, accurate translation is a masterpiece of pithy description and a wry account of human desires and foibles.

HB/Rs 450

The Seduction of Shiva
Tales of Life and Love

Translated by A.N.D. Haksar

Tales of love for all times

The god Shiva is utterly seduced by Mohini during
the churning of the ocean for nectar. A barber employs
wit and wile to win his wife back from the lustful
attentions of their king. The celestial nymph Urvashi
curses Arjuna when he spurns her. A woman caught
in adultery befools her elders with a religious ritual.
Refined, colloquial, romantic, cynical and satirical
by turns, these elegantly translated stories of erotic
love make a sustained argument for the secular ends
of life—of desire tempered with discrimination and
pleasure with restraint.

PB/Rs 299